INVITATION TO A VOYAGE

INVITATION TO A VOYAGE
FRANÇOIS EMMANUEL
TRANSLATED BY JUSTIN VICARI

DALKEY ARCHIVE PRESS
CHAMPAIGN / DUBLIN / LONDON

Originally published in French as *L'invitation au voyage* by La Renaissance du Livre, Brussels, 2003
Copyright © 2003 by François Emmanuel
Translation copyright © 2011 by Justin Vicari
First edition, 2011

Library of Congress Cataloging-in-Publication Data

Emmanuel, François, 1952-
[Invitation au voyage. English]
 Invitation to a voyage / François Emmanuel ; translated by Justin Vicari. -- 1st ed.
    p. cm.
 "Originally published in French as L'invitation au voyage by La Renaissance du Livre, Brussels, 2003"--T.p. verso.
 ISBN 978-1-56478-625-8 (pbk. : alk. paper)
 I. Vicari, Justin, 1968- II. Title.
 PQ2665.M53I6813 2011
 843'.914--dc22

                        2011029551

Partially funded by the University of Illinois at Urbana-Champaign, the National Lottery through Arts Council England, and by a grant from the Illinois Arts Council, a state agency

The publication of this work was supported by a grant awarded by the French Community of Belgium

www.dalkeyarchive.com

Cover: design and composition by Danielle Dutton, illustration by Nicholas Motte
Printed on permanent/durable acid-free paper and bound in the United States of America

The Invitation

You wrote me letters on fine paper, yellowed, nearly tanned by the sun, I ran them between my fingertips with a slightly superstitious bliss, as a child I used to tilt back the lid of the piano and caress the felt hammers, not making the slightest noise, for I have always taken pleasure in what goes unheard, crouching in expectation, vague speculation, we live in a time when the unknown is never completely unknown, the uncanny is smothered inside the mundane, when I began to read your letters I was captured instantly by the tone and the music, yet I understood nothing, I had to reach the last words so that in the rereading everything became clear in that flow of sentences that was wholly yours, conspicuously your voice, your voice that I have loved so much, that soul of yours which speaks to me today in the same way, rises up in me, from down where my very breath originates, from that area called solar, where we store our loves when they are precious, did I admit to you that I often forestalled the moment of reading your letter for several hours, as if to let its secret, so to speak, ripen, and to feel myself filled by those mysterious weights that lent my life here, my errands, my strolls, a certain weightlessness, you had written to me, the letter could stay in my inside pocket, the moment for opening it could be selected, deferred, I could devise the proper scenery for its reading, a public place of my choosing, café, streetcar, waiting room, a letter is so light, there is so little of the body in it that you exhaust yourself gathering in its details, its violet ink (gypsies, you said, put their children to sleep by slipping this color under their pillows), its texture, the paper's watermark, the scent from the unfolding sheets, doubtlessly hallucinated, reawakening the memory of your own scent, the rustling of the envelope when I held you there, still unopened, hidden in my inside pocket, reassuring me with the touch of your presence, in the secret bliss of being close to you while far away, in the imminence of reading you, strangely you never wrote my name as a salutation, you just started right in, you took up again an interrupted conversation, an abrupt monologue, composite, for there were leaps, ellipses, brusque gaps between your sentences, since your logic is feminine, you told me, it was men who invented logic, what good does it do to say what one knows, we, women, we speak only of what we can hold in our hands, if I'm not mistaken I recall your first letters as being longer, more descriptive, it seemed to me the invitation was not yet forthcoming, I could even believe our relationship would never again take anything but an epistolary course, better than nothing for the time being, until we inevitably lost contact altogether, you told me about your country, about the wind blowing in from Africa, the red earth, the rampart of olive trees beneath the sky's blue steel, flocks of sheep like seedbeds of raw silk across the hillsides, and I clearly recognized in all this your amorous palette of ochers, straw-yellows, sepias, mauves, those images that settled here on the grimy gray of these windowpanes, creating the space for an elsewhere, fragile, brightened by the sun, in the heart of this country that, as you knew, makes winter last from November to April, levels a white, overwhelming heat over July, and where we have only a few languorous evenings in June or September to feel the world's harmony as keenly as you, did I ever tell you how the winter twilights now and then turn the lights of your house crimson, until the wind grows warmer at the end of February, bears the promises of summer, the return of the first migrations, and news, I dared hope, news from your south, no, the invitation wasn't forthcoming in your first letters, you laid out the elements of your landscape, nothing more, the scenery of your existence, the way it flowed through your entire life, and I saw that carpet of hills where the shepherd called his flock, the melancholy of his long cries like trains in a bygone age, now and then you told a story, a tiny anecdote, one day's revelation, a chance visitation (Guglielmo, that visionary village idiot who lived in the church and would leave a melon, a squash under your stone steps), or you even inserted a haiku, a phrase drawn from something you had read, some sign from heaven, a poetic moment, and in them I no longer looked for anything but an invitation to commune a little with your solitude, though it occurred to you often enough to evoke the several days we spent together, you endlessly reread our brief affair, going over our little store of shared memories, which was how they found all their faults mysteriously magnified, thanks to your obsession with prolonging that period, teasing out our initial time together, always extending it, but run aground, finally, by your writing, rarefied by it, reduced to its essentials, a mere trace amid the threads of your gnawing evocations, your patient and singular memory-work, which, in these repetitions, in your re-reading, transforms the living past into a mythic one, perhaps in order to place the history we might have had upon a pedestal, a history that would still be ours, the past invoking the future, it occurred to me today, without the slightest doubt, that the invitation was implicit after all inside this clockwork return to the several days we spent together, to be sure barely a week, we were lovers from the second night on, it was love without end or perspective, strangely without sadness, a warm afternoon love in your room sifted with blue light, a love in which time was not measured, between the promenades and the eclipses of sleep, it was a harbor, a shelter for our bodies, we had no secrets from each other, we told each other our lives, our wounds, our fleeting joys, our voices appearing, words interlaced, along with their implications, in an uncanny ease of speech, you handled my language adroitly, sometimes with fractured, double meanings, a delicious inexactitude, a result of the differences in our respective tongues, though I still think our languages straining together amplified the cluster of meanings at hand, and why even bring up, here, the "false friends" of language, a strange expression, that might have confused us, we listened to how the words sounded, not what they meant, with the generosity of those who have nothing to hide or keep quiet, simply listening to and watching each other, I watched your face, your grace, your extremely delicate hands, your way of being in the world of objects and rituals that made up the inner workings of your household, I loved to watch you coming and going, unawares, singing, slicing bread, lighting a candle or setting the table, I loved that coziness where the threads of intimacy wove together, there was a curtain of thick cotton between the guest room and the bedchamber, I could only graze with words that other intimacy that unveiled itself within that penumbra, there where you gave your beautiful cry, there where our bodies burst onto the scene, wore themselves thin to show, as I see now, the intermingling of our souls, after making love we spoke as if in the evening of our lives, you told me your dreams and I tried to read them with you, to find the omens in them, to glimpse the lines of destiny aligning or diverging, to truly measure time, as though that were possible, in your letters too you told me certain parts of dreams, and I was in them, I accompanied you in the exploration of an island (what clearer metaphor for love?), the invitation was evident in those dreams that you had doubtlessly reconstructed upon waking and chosen for your letter with a degree of feminine subterfuge, or wisdom, I don't know, in response to those accounts of my own where dreams had wandered in, you quoted to me one day, my dream got devoured by yours, a landscape of absolute desire, I've forgotten the phrase exactly, I forgot my dreams, I forgot your part in them, I was less prompt in responding to you, our correspondence changed its tone, then you addressed snapshots or postcards to me, on the back of which your text grew brief, lapidary, *thought of you, thought of that song, dreamed about you again, dreamed of your city, why?* the unfinished nature of those sentences invited me to question you further, that way you never said *I*, the postcard pictures weren't innocent, four women laughing, straining wheat through their wicker tamis in a blonde light, where I live the workers are sad, you took, I'm sure of it, special care in picking out these peasant scenes, later a velveteen of bare hills crushed by sunlight, later still a view of the desert, the south, always the south, I saw our epistolary liaison taking yet another course, sometimes I told myself we were growing apart from one letter to the next, to make room for a weightless absence, an embellished memory, but something let me understand how the drying-up of our writing revealed another sort of movement, another exhibition, perhaps even that silence we knew whenever we entered the somewhat sacred chamber of our lovemaking, and which, with caresses giving way to words, our embrace giving way to caresses, the unfurling of images, the sensation of treading virgin earth, and the inanity, then, of everything that could be spoken, except for those rarest of words, knotted with breath, the simplest expression of the vow of love, the invitation seemed at first to be missing from those cards and yet, nonetheless, there it was, more than ever, you placed one finger upon my lips, you took me by the hand, and you lifted the curtain on the blue room, the last letter was a long time in coming, confused somehow I knew there wouldn't be any more, I waited for two days before opening it, toying with the thought that it would be the same as the preceding ones, fearful at the same time that everything would be inscribed there, terminated, accomplished, it was a white sheet folded in quarters, you had written nothing there but a few words, *the end of this endless patience has come, I await you.*

Love and Distance: A Fragmentary Report

"One wishes that everything was still to be said."
Louis Calaferte

Like a pointillist image, he explained with a wide sweep of his hand, and at that moment I thought he was crazy, he had that characteristic hint of brightness in his way of looking at me, that fixed and fevered something that didn't leave the slightest doubt, I had always thought there were all kinds of crazy people in the world, this guy without a doubt belonging to the peaceful variety, relatively normal, perfectly functional, but crazy nonetheless, rummaging through his narrow hallways all alone and pampering all his little obsessions, I thought that underneath his polite social façade, inside that luxurious office, all leather and mahogany, where he received me, behind his demeanor, a handsome older gentleman, his aesthete's manners (absurdly dressed though he was in a ratty wool bathrobe), he secretly cultivated a pleasant madness the way others do a vice or guilty passion. A madman, I thought, I was convinced of it, I watched him with his air of befuddlement, expanding on this particular hobbyhorse regarding women and the *pointillist image*, and knew he wouldn't have noticed in the least if I simply left the room. An old professor from this or that university, but then universities are great breeding grounds for madmen, I told myself, madmen with beards and diplomas, crazy driveling fools, scientific madmen, madmen photographed on the pedestals of renown, complete with togas, mortarboards, and academic palms, madmen stricken with a monomania either for words or for numbers, and this one's was evidently for words, what with his way of stopping right in the middle of a sentence to start all over again from the beginning, or to turn an idea perversely inside out, or to grasp hold of a word by chopping it up into syllables, like his own name, Hattgestein, Professor Hattgestein, that impossible surname he pronounced pedantically in three dry staccato measures, as if this alone were sufficient explanation.

And me, I saw myself rooted right there in the middle of his madness, nodding politely while I tried to understand where he was going with his *pointillist image*, how I should take his little attack of delirium, and, especially, trying to understand at what stage I had found myself pulled in by it. But after all, I told myself, my business, as hush-hush as it is, is a kind of service job, I have to deal with greed or morbid jealousy all the time, so why not go to work for a little low-key madness, especially since, judging by the Ming vases in the foyer, the Belle Époque furniture, and then the ravishing lute player who'd spied on me from behind a window on my way in, there was every reason to believe that his fees were by no means slight.

I want to know everything about this woman, he declared, then he corrected himself, no, in the final analysis, not everything, exactly, can one ever know everything about another person, I want details more than anything, miniscule details, insignificant to the eye but characteristic nonetheless, the kind of detail that makes you say, that is she, yes, that is she. He took his handkerchief out of his pocket and mopped his temples. Excuse my anxiety, he said, all of this is very out of the ordinary for me and I've had to overcome certain scruples before calling on someone in your line of work, fortunately I've heard nothing but good things about you, you come with excellent references, and moreover someone told me that you wouldn't take on just any assignment, which is a guarantee of your seriousness, things being what they are, which is why I've dared to take this step. Then he picked up the thread of his thought again, we shall speak then about details, trifling details, even if it seems futile to you, note them down, never lose them, hold tight to the tiniest observation, the next-to-nothings of her life, the nearly forgottens of her life, her childhood for example, what survives of her childhood may turn out to be of the highest degree of interest, approach her the way a naturalist approaches some marvelous and inexplicable phenomenon, let us be clear here, I am speaking of course about a naturalist from the last century, the only, the true naturalists, the ones who still mingled analysis with passion, science with the art of literature. Do you see what I mean? I didn't see, no, but I nodded as if I did. At the end of the interview he took an envelope out of his desk drawer and held it out to me in a protective way. This is the only photograph I have of her, he confided regretfully, I leave it with you for use in your investigation, please understand that I want nothing else of this nature, the truth I seek is more subtle and more intimate, be a painter or a poet, but above all not a photographer. He gave the barest hint of a smile. And make sure she is aware of nothing, it is for this reason in particular that I have appealed to someone in your line of work. On this last point I gave him every assurance. With a shaky hand he scribbled out my check, then he saw me out into the hall while leaning on the pommel of a cane whose metal tip jangled on the marble tiles with every step. Call me right away as soon as you have any little tidbits, he said, any little tidbits.

The image he gave me had been clipped out of a concert program, grainy from photocopying, and greatly enlarged. It was of a woman in three-quarters profile, her neck rather long, her hair done up in a bun, she looked at the camera with a slightly distant, slightly superior expression, but an afterthought, an imperceptible sensuality was visible upon her lips, as if the photographer had not been indifferent to her. This is a woman who says yes and who says no, I told myself, my curiosity piqued by her reserved and sensuous face, deliciously oblique. On the back of the photo Hattgestein had written her initials, *E. D.*, as well as the words *Philharmonic Orchestra*. Nothing, then, could have been simpler than purchasing a concert ticket for the Philharmonic, and getting a seat close enough to the musicians, in the second row of the orchestra circle for example, the spot would be ideal for a preliminary observation. All around me women exposed their bare backs bordered with stoles of raw silk, their eyes distractedly scanning the audience. By chance I was seated at precisely the same angle the photograph had been taken from, and from which I had only to lean slightly to the left in order to stalk, at my leisure, above the person seated in front of me, between the conductor's leg and the shoulder of my quarry's neighbor, the brief apparition of her face.

Sitting in front of her music stand, five or six meters away from me, she was perfectly faithful to her reproduction, haughty and unfathomable, wearing that industrious expression violinists have when they are squinting at their scores at the same time as turning a page, soon letting their right hands fall again, their bows extended along their legs, the same posture, at once alert and at ease, of a fencer between bouts. I noted these details, second violin, chest-nut-red hair, silver pin stuck through her bun, a slight and quasi-rhythmic nibbling of her lips when she leaned her head over the soundboard of her violin (he would like the precision of that word, soundboard), lifting her bow again for the attack. I also noted her white blouse with starched and modest collar, the silver locket matching the pin in her bun, her quick glances toward the conductor (her expression suddenly severe, and then one could sense her resolute character, that she was a real worker), her austere flat-heeled shoes, a slight arching of her left foot, tension and attention, the shudder of a rebellious lock of hair whenever she shook her head too sharply, a long black dress exactly like her neighbors', but hers bearing a tone-on-tone motif, a refined swerving away from the lockstep of uniform. Higher up her waist is slim, her breasts are perfect, two small apples (stay focused), her build is solid, her arms are long, her fingers hypnotic and acrobatic, a wedding band on the ring finger, a beauty mark just under the corner of her lip. Sometimes in the movement of her bow upon the strings, she inclined her head with half-closed eyes toward the melodic flow, at a low angle, a moment of grace and a kind of invitation to follow her, they were starting the andante of the Concerto for Violin and Orchestra, opus 64, by Felix Mendelssohn. Entranced by the opening bars I closed my eyes in turn and stopped taking notes. Then, when she stood up to bow at the end of the performance, I was surprised by her rumple-haired look, a vague glimmer of pleasure or even mischief, which I had not previously recorded in my notes. And yet, my qualms about neglecting to take down enough details was absurd, inasmuch as I thought I'd spotted my crazy old patron up in the balcony, from which vantage he could have seen everything just as well as I did. Still, he awaited further details about her from me. Tomorrow I would go to my office and continue conducting my investigation as usual, consulting secret files and employing a little discreet espionage. Soon we would see a great deal.

Her first name was Eve, she was thirty-eight years old, living in a residential neighborhood, a red-brick villa with large bay windows, an automatic garage door, a neatly mown lawn, and a rock garden of little flowers. She was married to a lawyer with a fairly prosperous practice and a gray SUV, 147 horsepower, kept in impeccable working order. The couple went to the tennis club on Thursdays from eight to ten, went skiing in February, to Mass at eleven o'clock on Sundays, and to the theater when they felt they could really splurge. Two children had been born from this sedate union, Arthur, age seven, and Amelie, age eight. Eve had been employed by the Philharmonic Orchestra for nearly a decade, part-time, a straight trajectory, good notices. She gave private lessons to young students on Wednesday afternoons. Her remaining time was plotted out rigorously from week to week, she did her grocery shopping on Thursdays, had friends over or else went out on Saturday nights, always took her dog for a walk on Sundays (thin slacks for these outings, red socks, a lofty bearing, her hair windblown). Good knowledge of English, likes sports, nature, and American comedies. Her favorite composer, Debussy. Perhaps I should leave that out, I told myself, Debussy and the American comedies. Most definitely I will note the black griffon with floppy ears, who, startlingly, responds to the name Bacchus, which name, that Bacchic disruption, is an anomaly among the perfect order of the details of her life. I will also note her tone of voice, as heard on her answering machine, a timbre that was grave but with an undertone of treble, shivering with a kind of silky aura, with just a shade of rapturous letting-go, albeit firmly restrained, perfectly mastered behind the formality of her message, We're not here right now, please leave a message after the tone. As for the rest, nothing, not the slightest step out of line, never the least infringement at any time, no guilty under-the-table activities. I must have underestimated the complexity of this case, I thought, while scheduling my next appointment with Hattgestein, and while talking to him on the phone, saying, look, I have a few tidbits already but nothing juicy.

Good work, he admitted, bent over my shoddy notes, at any rate I knew all this already. Then he lit up a little, except for the red socks, those red socks are new. Then he leaned back in his chair, pensive, as if hesitating between two thoughts. You tell me Debussy, he started in again, but which Debussy are you talking about? The Debussy of *Pelléas* or the Debussy of the piano works, the Debussy of a toccata or the Debussy of profound passion, and then you mention bay windows but you forget the drapes. Are they drawn, open, floral, opaque, how much light do they let through from inside? Such details as these may seem trifling but they are priceless (here we go, he's starting up again, I thought), don't take this the wrong way, I do understand the pains you go to, and I'm aware that the methods of your profession often lead to rather crude oversimplifications, appalling to be sure when it comes to shedding light on a precise matter, but in this situation nothing is precise, one's eye must always be on the alert, it's like fishing with a wide-mesh net, do you understand me? No, I was understanding less and less. Abruptly he stood and invited me to follow him into the next room, which resembled the gallery of a museum but must have been a salon, wallpapered with paintings by the masters, all plunged into a semidarkness. There, in one of the back corners, he illuminated a rather large canvas that I recalled having seen somewhere before. The figure on the left drew my attention right away, it was a young woman dressed in a flowing green gown, looking slightly to the side, perhaps dreaming, her lips carnal, slightly disdainful, one hand lifting up a fold of her dress, the other holding a wicker basket containing two white doves. The resemblance to the woman Eve was striking, in all the proportions of her face and especially her expression, cold, a bit distant, but perhaps discreetly complicit. It's only a copy, Hattgestein commented, nonetheless it is very faithful. You surely recognize the *Presentation at the Temple*, which is the right panel of the Saint Columba altarpiece by Rogier van der Weyden. See how this young serving girl looks right at us—there is only one other moment of intimacy so striking in all of Van der Weyden's work, a sketch hanging in the museum of Berlin, a portrait of his wife, they say. Yes, with the exception of God and certain majestic angels, the eyes even of background figures in the master's paintings are always lowered or turned away, as if a screen of piety or modesty must keep their gazes from breaking out of the diegetic space. Nevertheless, this young woman, perhaps the painter's lover, looks directly at us, making this part of the *Presentation* particularly arresting. Now step back from the painting, farther back, squint your eyes, imagine standing at a distance of fifty or a hundred meters, watch her blur, fade away, then come back to her, approach her calmly, keep coming closer, make contact with her, watch her move toward you, keep coming forward, do not stop advancing, keep going until you bump your head against the canvas, your face against hers, for she is at your eye level, then watch her blur into the material from which she is made, those brushstrokes which constitute her, take another step backward and find her again. You must not forget these fault lines in your perception, my employer told me later when we had returned to his office. Too far away she ceases to exist, too close she is no longer there. He held out his hand, trembling as when he had spoken to me of the *pointillist image*, but I no longer thought about his madness, I thought about the resemblance, I had a terrible urge to go back into the next room and verify that resemblance. It's not exactly a usual part of my procedure, I told him, but if we want to make some progress I will have to establish contact with her. He frowned, pondered a while, then finally accepted the idea. Perhaps music will furnish you with a pretext for getting to know her, he proposed while seeing me out, it figured among your references, I was told you were not insensitive to it.

So close, at such a distance that I could have touched her, she was indeed very beautiful, perfumed with L'Air du Temps, a little bit stiff in her black turtleneck, and intrigued that a man my age wished to take violin lessons.

Finally she buried her astonishment by leafing through a little gilt-edged datebook to arrange our first rendezvous. Leaving the villa, the most I dared to admit to myself was that the job was an intriguing one, I was moving in some elite circles, and maybe, just maybe, I was feeling something. Doubtless an effect of L'Air du Temps, I told myself while straightening the lapels of my coat, let's stay professional. That day I learned two or three supplemental details, there was a collection of blue glassware, small bottles, flasks, and phials, aligned on the bureau in her hallway (nothing unusual about that), menthol cigarettes hidden away in the leather handbag from which she had produced her datebook, fur-lined slippers which didn't match her elegant black leotard and her general, rather gymnastic presence (hop hop hop, back and forth, here I am), and finally her slight show of annoyance when the dog started barking from behind a door (ah, Bacchus, who emblematized in himself alone all the secret savagery of the household). Leaving, I kept hearing her velvety intonation in my head, her way of muffling her words in her breath, and I stopped by the library to plunge again into the *Presentation at the Temple*, again finding the resemblance intact and fascinated by the fact that this young serving woman looked at me without looking at me, depending on the angle I stood at. Eve must also have suffered from a slight myopia, in her house I caught her squinting at me from afar, casting an uncertain look, as if vaguely surprised, unless this had to do with something else, something in her eye, a passing presentiment, but since this sign was indecipherable, I didn't believe it would be useful to mention it.

Six days later, the door on the left-hand side of her foyer opened onto a library with a round table pushed into one corner and two Louis Philippe armchairs, one for her and one for me. That day she wore a turquoise suit and conscientiously inquired about my motives, my background in musical matters, and the possibility of my acquiring an instrument for practice. I furnished appropriate responses, three years of sol-fa, one year of violin long ago, my regret at having had to stop, and the desire, yes the desire, to one day be able to play a Hungarian or Scottish dance solely for the pleasure of rekindling a little nostalgia and entertaining kids at get-togethers. Very serious, she noted down my words (but what had I even said?) in a little spiral notebook, on the page under my name. And while she took notes, I glanced sidelong at some new details, the pattern of stripes on her jacket, the slender silver necklace that sparkled between two buttons of her blouse, or the fleeting way her tongue glided between her lips, a charming indication that she was concentrating. On the floor there was a fire-red Oriental rug, against the wall a bookcase with some beautiful spines in faux-leather (a teach-yourself-to-be-a-great-cook manual and then the complete works of Balzac, thanks to some promotional offer), two engravings perfectly aligned, and wallpaper with a motif depicting flowers in rain. Not a single false note, I told myself, not the slightest sign of sloppiness, while she recovered her official smile and, having included me in her weekly schedule, already seemed eager for me to leave. I will need to have, I thought, a great deal of patience. A great deal of patience, she echoed in agreement, music requires no less, and, she added, not without malice, the will to overcome.

Thus, everything was frozen within this single immutable setting, my appointment time was always the same, I stumblingly recited si la sol sol fa mi, from start to finish, three times, from the top again, I plucked the string with one curled finger, under her indulgent eye I produced a huffing, muddy sound, si la sol, once again, toward the end of the first staff of this Scottish scherzo which she herself had crossed at a dash in a few sublime seconds, inviting me afterward to place my big feet in her dancer's steps. The decor never changed, Balzac and the blue glassware, only her outfits varied from lesson to lesson and sometimes her eyes flashed with a brief approbation, nuanced with condescension, even as I was doomed by the child prodigy with the splendid violin case who waited out the exhausting end of my si la sol sol in the hallway. Nothing ever really departed from the order of each lesson, one day she was slightly more weary or distracted, her hair more rumpled, another day she made a gesture to correct the position of my violin, but a sharp gesture, without warmth, purely didactic, and sometimes Bacchus whined behind the door, a downpour streaked the windowpane, an angel passed overhead with no consequence. At the end of the sixth lesson, as I wrote out her check, the amount of which was exactly one tenth of what Hattgestein had paid me, I thought that all of this would never be worth even that little bit of money which was slipping, momentarily, and only through my mercenary intervention, from him to her. Nevertheless, my patron still seemed to believe in the progress of my investigation. It is her middle-class cocoon, he asserted, we must wait for it to split open, and I see the opening has begun to sprout. What Hattgestein didn't seem to see were how few details I brought him from that point on, as if my tool of observation were somehow out of whack, secretly crippled by that spell which the object of my study had wrought upon me. And I hurriedly left the old professor in order to practice the opening notes of the Scottish dance, imagining this would please my *belle dame*, that she would lavish her smile upon me, that she would bring her lips close to me while murmuring softly, You surprise me, Monsieur, your progress is delightful. For I found that the less she gave, the more she melted into her decor, and the more ensnared I was in the trap of her splendid impassivity. This woman is a tableau vivant, Hattgestein had warned me, and the old man now became more friendly toward me, took up his cane to invite me on a tour of his collections, an African Venus, a Kali idol whose neck he made me caress, an Aphrodite languishing on a divan, a bathing beauty by Harunobu, and, for the finale, the young woman with the doves. Beauty, he explained, is like falling light, certain faces drink in this light more than others, but at bottom they are completely unaware of it, beauty answers to the physical laws of light, diffusion, reflection, diffraction, beauty is like the rime that melts away at one's touch, only those who know how to look can seal a pact with it, beauty is always traveling, one must approach it without baggage. And he clasped my shoulder paternally, persuaded that I was carrying out his scheme to the letter, unaware or feigning ignorance of the fact that we were each absorbed by a different score, he ordering me, get closer to her, since I'm paying you to watch her, and she commanding me, hold the bow without trembling, since you're paying me to teach you, and I, whenever she turned her beautiful face toward the window and I thought I detected a furtive roughness in her voice, a slight unease in her eyes, I who believed I was leading the dance, si la sol sol fa mi.

Luckily, things worked out so that I didn't need to arrange my own opportunity. Miraculously escaping from his kitchen, Bacchus placed his big affectionate snout and his dirty paws on my raincoat while I was seated in the hall, docilely waiting for my seventh lesson. Dismayed, Eve briskly sent the animal packing, was profuse in her apologies, and led me into her bathroom (teeming with flowers on the walls, scented with lavender) to try to clean away the spots. Thanks to this unexpected contretemps, our conversation strayed from the well-marked paths of musical pedagogy. Bacchus must have smelled my cat, I ventured without laughing (pure dramaturgy, I own no pet), she looked up, intrigued, and while scrubbing my raincoat, allowed herself to digress with me on the subject of the ancestral hostility between dogs and cats, cats in cat-holes, and from cat-holes to the habits of domesticated felines, wandering a little through the sort of small talk shared by neighbors just beginning to get to know each other. And what's your cat's name? she asked me in the mirror's reflection. *Miss Phi-phung-li*, I answered. She nearly burst out laughing. I'll bet, she said, wiping her fingers, that the affections of Miss Phi-phung-li are less likely to stain. We went back into the library, ready to attack the seventh lesson, but now possessed, myself as much as her, of a very distinct inclination to dissipation, perhaps even

the subdued need to giggle. After a wheezing recapitula-
tion of the Scottish dance and since by extraordinary luck
the little violin prodigy was late that day, she brought up
my cat again. And where did that name come from, Phi-
phung-li? she made so bold as to enquire. She's Burmese,
I answered very seriously. Eve looked at me, perplexed.
The conversation started up again, between sidesteps and
veiled confessions, along the lines of a game, which, little
by little, imposed its own rules. All at once she was curious about the habits of my cat and stared at me with an
ironic sort of look as if she could see the depth of my lie in
my eyes. Miss Phi is a black empress, and I am her servant,
I said, she takes her naps on my silk pillows and dines only
on smoked salmon (one slight error, Burmeses are choco-
late brown). And you never tire of her whims? Eve asked
me with her cheeks reddening. I am, by nature, accom-
modating, I announced. This time Eve could not suppress
a very wide smile, and she chewed her lips, smitten and at
the same time making fun of me, evidently desiring that
I go on talking about my cat's habits and thus a little bit
about myself. Was I only the servant of Miss Phi-phung-li?
Did I not offer my services as well to those big tomcats
who surely couldn't help but come sniffing around her? I

replied that the odd hours necessary in my work as a *photographer* allowed her more than enough time to attend to her lovers. Eve looked away and seemed to blush.

From that moment on, the lessons took a different turn. Before commencing, Eve would ask for news of my cat, and then, once this little ritual was exhausted, would invite me to open the score to the marked page, to hold my note with conviction, though not without a kind of menacing, even lunatic laughter lurking around us, as if she knew I had come to her for some hidden purpose and that I knew that she knew, and that, finally, she knew that I knew she was not fooled. Once the violin was put away, and while Bacchus whined jealously from behind the door, Eve allowed herself to take up the game of light, exquisite conversation with me, and I tried to keep the amused flicker of her blue-green eyes alert, from Miss Phi we digressed to my pretended work, photography, a difficult art, capturing fragile moments, and she believed me without believing me, letting herself circumvent politely, while I allowed myself to find her charming, always the same and always different, black or fuchsia, haloed with flowers or pastels, one day more teasing, tender, sensuous, another day more inclined to laugh, tossing back her head, touching my arms as she cackled in that L'Air du Temps which enveloped us both like lovers on a boat drifting from the shore. Everything became a pretext for something else, wait I have to tell you, wait I was thinking, wait we'll speak of this some other day, I'm sure you'll be crazy about it, and thus was woven a love story like millions of other stories being woven at that same moment out in the world. I forgot Hattgestein, who had paid for our boat and was growing smaller and smaller on the shore. Out of professional ethics and to make the little game harder, I brought my patron two or three tidbits about Eve all the same, she prefers the mountains to the sea, tea to coffee, Debussy to Ravel, and I've confirmed that her violin is a Mougenot, it was given to her by her husband on her thirtieth birthday, as for her eyes I can't decide between green leaning toward blue or blue leaning toward green, anyway it depends on the light and she wears contact lenses. But still, but still, balked the old man whose good humor was starting to darken, who became strangely nervous, sullen, began muttering, I am no longer seeing very clearly, no I no longer see her, something is not right with the terms, it is not she whom I see. Me, I see her very well, I thought while pocketing his check, I see vividly her small breasts protruding under her blouse, and her legs crossing and uncrossing under her dress, and her chestnut-red hair shining in the light, and her thighs rolling, and her pert little buttocks lifting, and the outline of her lips growing wider, yes growing wider, when she becomes innocently enraptured, good, that's very good, I'm proud of you. At the end of the twelfth lesson (very little of the Scottish dance that day), she hurled herself forward abruptly, actually I have one small request to make, would you have any objection to enlarging some childhood photos for me? She was breathless all of a sudden. Not the least objection in the world, I answered her, I can even show you how to do the enlargements yourself, you're teaching me your art so patiently, I would be very happy to initiate you into my own craft in turn. She was completely at a loss about this but didn't say no, even went so far as to refuse to let me pay her that day. This will be an exchange of services, your lesson for mine, and she added with an exhalation, since we're friends.

What happened next was straight out of any number of books. Deep in the cellar where I developed my compromising negatives, L'Air du Temps mingled with the acrid odor of my chemicals, our hands groped in the red penumbra, we brushed against each other without touching, I felt her hair sweep my cheek, and the caress of her mohair sweater, and her voice very close by, mouth dry from the sensation of something about to happen, and then, when the first features of a face began to appear on the gloss of the paper that floated to the surface of my developing bath, under the cover of this sudden miracle, she let her head fall upon my shoulder, and all at once gave the sign that I could kiss her, she brutally turned herself volte-face, melted against my body, our lips found each other, then our hands, mad with impatience, were undoing sashes and belts, and here was this violin woman pressed fully against me, haughty and trembling, as was her nature, Eve from head to toe, Eve exultant before the red bulb of my darkroom, and tossing out little aspirated laughs, shallow, like a swimmer taking in air several times before plunging back down into her deep waters, at the moment when I told myself, this hiccup of love, this song, I possess it, it is her gift to me, that detail canceled out all the others, I grabbed it and held on.

With her six- or seven-year-old eyes, her big toothless grin, she was also laughing in her photograph, turning her head in front of a row of houses, white as the sky and her skin, for the picture had gotten overexposed. Elsewhere in a bathing suit she sat upon a knoll of sand as if it were a throne, and then, on the same acre of beach, she held up a shovel in one hand, standing next to a naked little boy. These are shadows of time, exhaled Hattgestein enigmatically, then he took out his magnifying glass and, bent double, plunged again into methodical contemplation of these snapshots, his eyes only a few centimeters away from them. Afterward he looked up and stared at me strangely, but without looking directly at me, it seemed, he began to ask me all sorts of questions. When do these photos date from? What year exactly? Where were they taken? In what city? And why there? And why that year? And who was behind the camera? And who was this little boy? Was he her younger brother? And what was this younger brother's name? I told him what I could, I embroidered the single mention of time and place scrawled in pencil on the back of one of the photos, *La Panne, July 19* . . . He didn't seem to listen to me at all, every question led into another as if he was seeking thereby to exhaust the impact of the images. At one point he stopped cold and gathered up the photos with an emphatic air and stuffed them into a leather briefcase that contained all the pages of my report, then his eye returned to light on me in silence, this time he truly seemed to be looking at me. You're beginning to see? I asked, hoping to distract him from his malaise. All I see is the impossibility of seeing, he said softly, I see these little things that you bring me and because of them, precisely because of them, I cannot see her anymore, she disappears behind these thousand details I have solicited and which have now begun to obstruct my view. Since the moment I enlisted you, one could say that she has been lost, her image no longer resonates the way it did, and now when I watch her in concert I think about what you have told me, these stories, these unilluminating details, yes, it seems to me that at a single blow her enigma has become pointless, she takes her bow, she vanishes into the wings, I cannot see her anymore. He took a deep breath. It is evidently a problem of method, he went on as if overwhelmed, one believes one is looking through a wider and wider lens, but one sees only the lens, the irisations, the dust motes on its surface, when I was an art critic I was always knocking my head against this decisive problem, how to speak about Flemish painting, how to speak about the blue of the virgin's cloak without forever erasing the color behind the word that qualifies it? Leaning toward me, he continued in a very low voice, try to understand, Monsieur, a woman looks at you one evening after a Mahler concert, a woman crosses your path by chance, for two or three seconds she looks in your direction as if staring into the abyss, as if she knew that you were there precisely to recognize her and so waited for you to take a step toward her, that first step which you could never take, never, but nonetheless she calls to you, leaving you there voiceless, obsessed with her, condemned to go back endlessly to that place where your eyes met, and to attend her concerts every evening if need be, because you cannot stop thinking that whenever she happens to look up at the audience she might be looking for you, until the moment when in despair you appeal to a private detective, lamentably deceiving yourself about the efficacy of this stand-in, for this man is not from the same world, in spite of what you have been told about his professional skills or his pretended affinity for music, and little by little you discover that what he gives you to look at simultaneously prevents you from seeing her, you come to realize that these innumerable details that ought to initiate you into the mystery of this woman only serve to thicken it to such a degree that one day you see nothing more than those details, your view is definitively clouded over, this man has come to stand between you and her, he has made a screen out of his entire body, you no longer see anything but him. The old professor stared at me with a terrible fixity, I don't know if he was waiting for a response. Finally, I heard myself stammer that now I better understood what he wanted, I believed I better understood. What do you understand? he roared. I answered, the blue of the virgin's cloak. His eyes grew wide, he raised his hand as if I had just uttered a frightful blasphemy, he bolted to his feet, paced nervously around the room while letting his cane chime upon the tiles, came back and sat down in his chair, picked up the leather briefcase and, trying to regain his composure, stared at me once more, and stared, and stared. Let's try again, he said, his eyes suddenly far away, his voice trembling, but above all do not ruin anything, promise me that you will not ruin anything. I promised him. He saw me to the foyer without a word, closed the four deadbolts of his door behind me. A total madman, I told myself, shouldering through the gate of his palatial estate, definitely a total madman.

On the other hand, life opened its wide arms to me, love lost nothing for being made to bide its time. When I called Eve to make sure of our next rendezvous, she answered me in a very low voice, breathless, that she would wait for me as expected on the day of my lesson. The lesson, our thirteenth to be precise, took place in a sort of discomfort, an impetuous rush. The curtains drawn, we very quickly abandoned the first measures of the Scottish dance for other transports hardly less musical, the scraping of the Louis Philippe armchair and then the chirping of the castors on the round table which rolled and thumped against the baseboard in a frenzy, while Bacchus squealed like mad under the door and Eve let out, indiscriminately, her broken little cries of ecstasy. The doorbell then the dull thud of the front door brought us abruptly back to our senses, obliging us to get dressed again quickly and hide in the bathroom, which luckily was adjoining, while I grabbed my violin to conceal the sound of running water, recovering like a robot the fixed path of si la sol that still resonated with her song of interrupted love. You must go to the very end of the note, she said gravely while taking up her place again in three-quarters profile on the chair and pulling a little pocket mirror from her bag to touch up her make-up. I performed for several minutes, she checked to make sure everything was in order, the curtains, the walls, the folds of her dress, and within this order finally restored, made immutable again, I was able to whisper in her ear that conditions were not optimal and it would be better to see each other at my place, in the tranquility of my private rooms. Monday from three to four, she proposed while chewing her lip, she had dreamed about it. We exchanged a brief kiss to end the session.

From that moment on, the lessons took place at my house, according to an unalterable ritual, five past three, she gave two short bright rings of the doorbell, five past three, we were nearly naked in the consecrated environment of my bedroom, her clothes neatly folded on a chair, and already we were thrilling each other's skin with a thousand caresses as we slowly set out to sea on the skiff of my bed, while the sweet breeze of L'Air du Temps swelled the sail of love, our conversation reduced then to little nothings, interjections, stammered and muffled invitations (yes, yes, that's it, yes, yes, more) until in the light that sifted through my greenish curtains Eve arched her whole body and hurled out her sublime final notes. Then I saw us floating together a meter above the mattress before falling back down in slow motion in a shower of gold dust. Then our bodies began to loosen their embrace, to caress each other more distractedly, she breathed with ease while turning her back to me, languorously coiling herself around a secret she had not shared, let a vague urge to talk come back to her, talk about everything and nothing, my bed whose squeaky springs would need to be replaced one day, her husband whom she said she loved but who was not very gifted in the arts of love, there as in business driven only to get things done quickly, and on the road the rest of the time. At three fifty she stretched her long legs out from under the sheets and into my bathroom for a series of

46

ceremonial ablutions, then I watched her get dressed again, gracious and always very technical, putting on her nylon stockings, buttoning her blouse with her fingertips, brushing her hair back and skillfully straightening the bobby pins in her bun. During these preparations she asked me why I watched her that way, and I invariably answered her, I love to see how it's made, the beauty of a woman. We ended with the kiss of longtime lovers, it was five past four.

But at root, how was the beauty of a woman made? At that moment when, half dressed, she noticed my eyes upon her, I always realized the same thing, that she was piecing her mystery back together and would then begin to slip away from me. I realized that she whom I believed I possessed was in fact someone else, someone who'd come to switch bodies with her, and already nearly gone. In the ebb tide of desire I felt my heart clench up and perhaps the ache of a profound misunderstanding. Out of the blue I also thought of Hattgestein.

It's strange that my memory holds so few recollections from that time, I hear her two rings of the doorbell, I see her hurriedly shutting my door behind her (bundled in a beige scarf, setting down a basket with provisions on the table and unbuttoning her sable-colored cloak), then she reappears nude in the doorway of my bathroom and starts to get dressed again. In between these two moments we have played our part in the great seesaw of the world, deep within the starry night, wallowing in the luminous mire of these confines, we spent our energy crossing endless forests of lianas, trapping the bull, the tiger, the Minotaur, in a melee from which we returned dazed and amnesiac, she put on her nylon stockings, her blouse, her skirt, she became perfect again. Sometimes in the little time we had, beforehand or afterward, we happened to talk a little about ourselves (she hated her new maestro, her husband was in Singapore, they were planning to build a veranda), in short she lost herself in these ephemeralities, then changed her mind, I know, this isn't very interesting, and threw herself into my arms again to pour out a long Lethe-like kiss. We are blank spaces in each other's lives, I thought at those moments, we come together but only in the bottomless pit of Monday three-to-four. Besides, my professional expertise could not help but detect the subtle precautions she took so that no one would notice our arrangement, parking her car as far away as possible, never lingering around my door, always having an alibi ready. And especially no presents, no letters, she insisted, they always turn up at the bottom of a purse or a drawer, my husband is happy the way he is, what he doesn't know can't hurt him.

And us, were we happy? That question would be better left to others. Something had faded, it's true, perhaps something was already lost, but what good would it have done us to admit it? Over time our bodies no longer surprised each other, the double ring of Monday at five no longer thrilled me as it had in the beginning, I wanted novelty and risk (one night in the Central de Trouville, one day on the tracks of the Paris metro) but the slightest hint of risk made her vicious, she yearned for something different that was no longer me exactly, she dreamed of a voyage with her husband to Cancún or Acapulco, we skipped a lesson without too many regrets, some disenchanted remarks salted our conversations after lovemaking, hey I thought you had a better sense of humor, you should get new carpets, so where is your famous Burmese cat? oh okay so that's what's known as art photography, oh okay. And then we began to irritate each other, pleasing and displeasing each other with our annoyances, squabbling just to pass the time, the boat put out to sea but the wind no longer blew very hard, her body was restless under my caresses, little by little the bedsprings gave out, the song of love grew wheezy, she no longer laughed. Watching her back turned away on my bed in the dull light, her thick chestnut-red mop spilled across her naked skin, I thought she had been leaving me ever since that day she took her little gilt-edged datebook out of her bag with an anxious look, I thought I had passed over to the other side but now I no longer saw anything but her curves and outlines, I must have missed something. At best, she remarked one day while taking a menthol cigarette out of her purse, at best our affair would be a short story. Let's try to give it a good ending, I proposed while forcing a smile. She didn't look up. The last time was like the others, hardly any less banal. Watching her get dressed again, I surprised myself by thinking that even this little ceremony had become ordinary, incidentally I asked her about the blue in Flemish paintings and she raised her head, intrigued. Then

I asked her if she knew Professor Hattgestein, she shrugged and muttered, that old loon.

The next day I went back to the old loon's house to put an end to the whole business. At first Hattgestein eyed me suspiciously. I told him, I don't have anything more, Monsieur, I don't have anything more to bring you about her, and he seemed relieved. He spoke these words, your failure is doubtlessly my fault, my young friend, you did not understand the primary issue, but how could you have? This is a matter where we often deceive ourselves. In spite of my reluctance he insisted on giving me a final check, for the balance, he said, paid in full. I went away with the impression that he hadn't told me everything, but what did it matter? With the money from the check I purchased a long dress made of blue chintz (lapis lazuli, I specified to the terrified saleslady) and had it sent to Eve's house anonymously. That evening a black cat came and perched on the outside sill of my window, striking a pose seated over the void and watching me through the glass with a distant stare of despair.

Life likes to move in circles and it happens that a few forgotten photographs are floating in my developing bath. Some time had passed, my practice violin was gathering dust under my wardrobe, and from that whole affair I retained only the sensation of having brushed up against music, painting, and grace, and being found unworthy of such associations. Three years later, I found Hattgestein's obituary by chance in a local newspaper. The text, bordered in black, stated that he had once been a professor of quantum physics and the founder of a short-lived art review for the blind. And that same chance placed his little lute player and his Harunobu print in my path, at the back of a secondhand shop, in the shade of haggard old clocks, amid a jumble of ewers and umbrella stands. I searched everywhere for his copy of *Presentation at the Temple* with the young girl and her doves, but she was nowhere to be found. There was nothing else to do but go back to the Philharmonic, using all manner of legitimate reasons as a pretext. To master an obsession, I told myself, as a tribute to Hattgestein, or to understand, who knows, with the backward-looking perspective of time, what I had not understood then. Eve was there, in her usual place, seated in half profile on her chair, as beautiful and as sure of her beauty as ever, sometimes casting toward the orchestra circle that same haughty and mysterious look that made all things possible again. After the concert I was the last one remaining in the hall but something prevented me from going backstage, I thought that I couldn't yield to this kind of impulse where she was concerned, but had to earn each retied thread one at a time, to start everything over again, patiently, from the beginning.

Since then, I've gone back fairly often, and she never varies, the programs vary, the soloists vary, sometimes the grand orchestra cedes its stage to a smaller ensemble, but she is always there, sometimes wearing my blue dress. Sometimes I would like to cross the steps that separate us, I contemplate opportunities, introductions, little scenarios of conquering her again, but I know that this is all in vain, on this field the game has already been played out, I've played my hand. So when the choir of violins swells, when the wind of the music levels that mass of strings, bending as a single body, when the face of Bach or Mendelssohn stands illumined, I watch her half-closed eyes and try to see her by fleeting traces, like an apparition. It isn't easy, I must erase from my memory what I know about her, especially what I think I know, those few, too visible dregs our affair left behind. At some of these moments, if the music is propitious, it happens that I see her stand apart from the other musicians and claim the enchantment of the piece for herself alone. Then I think again about the young woman with the doves, whom Rogier loved, whom he brought to his atelier then dressed up as a royal serving girl so that she could mingle incognito among his wealthy patrons, Mary, Joseph, or Simon, while stamping her with the seal of a look in his direction, what stands between you and I, watches us. The emotion finds itself again nearly intact when, coming home from the concert, I put an old LP of Mendelssohn's opus 64, for example, on my turntable. And when the needle, having reached the end of a side, does not return to its point of departure but keeps pounding rhythmically against the emptiness like muted waves, I hear the sound of Hattgestein's cane upon his marble tiles, and I linger for a second in his strange company.

The Cartographer's Waltz

To Pascal Allard, who loves antique valises.

"What is a frontier? Our books teach us that it is a dream born from the union of geography and history."
Bertrand Visage

I left a country in the belief that I would never return to it. I erased it from my memory. For years I dwelled in this intended forgetting, this feigned ignorance, until, through no will of my own, the forgetting itself was forgotten. After that I no longer turned down assignments that sent me back to wander around those same places again. The assignments were strictly routine. They concerned the collection of samples, cartographic inquiries. The administration put me up in a hotel for a few days, I rubbed elbows with gloomy businessmen, and I filed my report.

On maps where I simply had to fill in blanks, the job was nothing more than numbers and legends. The numbers didn't mean anything, and there's nothing to tell about the legends. With a woman who came to enliven a few of my solitary nights, I called myself a geographer, in the manner of Nuño García de Toreno, and I invented for myself a homeland far away.

Was it really a lie? I didn't believe so. Childhood has no homeland, I told myself, I could have been born in the south, from redder clay, this didn't alter any of my memories, the taste of horseradish on my tongue, a garden framed inside a dormer window, a blue veranda flooded with moonlight, or some other tender, cruel, exquisite sensation that one passes through recklessly, as a child, and which one later regards as a happiness destroyed.

Nevertheless, that same happiness, which haunted me, dazzled me with its occult allure. And, tracing circles that grew closer and closer to overlapping, I prowled in spite of myself along the outskirts of this kingdom (as if these were walled gardens, or uncharted territories) supposedly on behalf of the mindless, desperate jobs I consented to perform.

Winter had been long, but now we were into the first warm days. They had sent me to check on lichen in a northern sector. An exhausting task, I had to divide the region into squares, take samples at marked places, report them on a map. Some lichen species are more sensitive than others to acid rain, they get covered in spots, crumble at your touch, die a slow, agonizing death. A preliminary map of ailing lichens had been compiled twenty years previously. It was not particularly comforting.

The zone I had to investigate was situated within a triangle that united Lille, Arras, and the northernmost point of the hexagon of France. In Arras a very pure blue sky bathed the houses of the vast public square in a maritime clarity. This light must have stirred up memories for me, because that morning I was lethargic and restless, I walked to my own interior time and everything felt possible to me. At a certain distance away, on the far side of the nearly deserted square, there was a man staring at the ground, then at the sky, following the row of housefronts, then turning at a ninety-degree angle and starting his little game all over again. He wore a bright outfit, with a wide-brimmed felt hat on his head, and the cane that ornamented his frame didn't seem to serve much of a purpose, as his gait was brisk. I wanted to approach him but some shyness held me back, a foreboding perhaps, the most authentic encounters are often preceded by a feeling of wariness.

He appeared again that afternoon, on a guided tour of the underground city. He was old but his bearing was still lively, insouciant, aristocratic. We trailed the guide at some distance. He asked me for my arm on one of the stairways leading down to those calcareous chambers, planted with giant pilasters. It's like a memory, he exhaled with a smile, it's more and more ancient the farther down we go. And yet this British installation from World War I reaches far deeper than the cathedral above us, which dates back to the French Revolution, I teased. The man stopped short. Who are you? he asked. Posed likewise by his dark eyes, the question resounded through me like a who-am-I? The man called himself Tyler, Alexandre Tyler. That was how we came to meet each other twelve levels underneath the city. At the fourteenth there was water, and this, indeed, seemed like a true immersion into memory.

By chance or good fortune he was staying, like me, at the Hôtel de l'Univers, a beautiful, antique lodging house that had sold its soul to purchase, at great expense, a third star. Tyler seemed to live there at his leisure, and I confess that after meeting him I forgot my ailing lichens. He caught on quickly that I was, let us say, a cartographer, and this fact seemed to amuse him. The reason for his amusement is clear to me now, but at the time I didn't understand it. No more than I was able to understand his personality, over-all. Spontaneous, at once forthcoming and oblique, capable of dazzling moments and long, petrified silences both. Except for the fact that he occupied Room 35 and break-fasted in the English way, really I knew nothing about his life, his former career remained a mystery, like his presence in Arras and the meaning of his solitary game that morning in the vast square, staring at the sky, the ground, and the row of housefronts while carrying out secret experiments or performing the imperceptible coded movements of an oriental dance, doubtless very much like the same ballet I offered to him from afar, in passing, as he watched me circle my perimeter, breaking off a dried-up lichen from a rock or going down on one knee to transcribe a number in my cross-ruled notebook.

Our entire acquaintance would play itself out under this sign, this mirroring, albeit a distant mirror, an enigmatic mirror. The old Englishman, moreover, was nonpareil in his ability to reflect back every question I asked him. No problem, he was born in Ipswich, Suffolk, but I, where was

I born? Where had he learned our language so well (with that suave roll in the throat that still lost nothing of its own accent)? But a language gives itself to whomever wishes to take it, he replied as if stung. It uses seductions and illusions to draw you in. Reticences too, sometimes. French is, as you know, a feminine language. For me she was a lover. For you a mother, I presume.

For me a mother? No, I've never thought of her that way. Then he smiled, looking at me askance like an old Zen master or a sly psychoanalyst, reading me like an open book, on this page my urge to run away and hide, on that one my compulsive desire to prowl around in circles, which is why, my young man, you'll find yourself sketching maps one day.

Even as my questions became more precise, more pointed, he still gave me the slip, his cane skipping about in the air. But I don't know any more than you, he exclaimed, then digressed into topics that had nothing, or next to nothing, to do with anything. Take navigation in the seventeenth century, for example, he said. You're going from Brest to Siam. From east to west the rate of declination changes by several degrees but you are unaware of this. The tiniest scrap of metal, the smallest rifle throws off the compass reading, firelight is all you have to see by. To mark your speed you have at your disposal only a knotted rope and an hourglass. To tell time you entrust yourself to a pendulum that loses one hour per day. Thus, there is nothing left for you but the seamarks, vaguely indexed on a map, here a coral reef, there a bear-shaped rock, and if you are far out to sea, nothing but imperceptible signs, a bird who comes to catch his breath on the masthead, a certain shade of the water, a certain sweetness of the air. In those days, travel was an adventure. What did you want to ask me about, again?

Your voyages, Mr. Tyler.

Arras is my voyage, for the time being. Where are we?

The quay of the old riverbank.

Good.

It was a gushing April. Toward noon clouds of white silk began to invade the sky and the wind picked up, a pretext for telling stories. There was a certain night, he said, in the desert, one night in the clutches of Notos, when the wind was so fierce it dulled the blades of their weapons, and

Alexander's army found itself lost. All reference points buried in sand, his guides haggard, rambling, retracing their paths, trying to reinvent their trail from nothing. Two crows, fortunately quite strong, blacker than misery, came out to show the way. When night fell the men regrouped around their raucous caws as around the word of God, and thereon from night to night until the oasis of Ammon. Where are we right now?

Rue des Agaches.

And where are we going?

To the Governor's Garden.

Good, very good. It's lucky you're a cartographer.

He weighted that word with a full measure of malice. I ventured to respond, you know too many things not to have had such a career yourself. He contented himself with smiling. I prodded a little, surveyor, geographer, historian?

Surveyor, he sighed. But we've already walked for three hours, and I'm tired from counting the steps.

In the Governor's Garden we sat down not far from a ruined monument showing two figures in polite conversation, one dressed in eighteenth-century attire, with doublet and puffed breeches, the other in a suit and bowtie, both decapitated. I gently asked my question again. Tyler shook his head in silence. Then he said, I mapped all the fountains in downtown Vancouver. I mapped the silences of London. My work resembles yours, in some respects, making a grid of the city, noting the acoustic pollution in each unit, recording them on a map. Louder than a hundred decibels is deep red, less than twenty is very pale pink. Needless to say there was very little pink, barely one or two spots, in the middle of Kensington Gardens or else in a couple of the soundproofed suites at Claridge's. This was all meant for a meditator's topographic guide to the city, but the publisher went bankrupt.

He stared at me with a flicker of amusement.

I don't know anymore if I should believe you, I said.

Think what you like. Doubtless our areas of investigation are not the same. You work on the surface, I in the depths. Deep cartography is a wholly inexact science. Recall, for example, the map of the Arras tunnels during the First World War. For the benefit of navigation, it had been necessary to name all the passageways that led between the great arcades. An old English tradition is to name a military installation after cities. Here, then, at ten meters underground, a disturbing geography, Liverpool juxtaposed with Edinburgh, Kent bordering the state of Wales, and here and there fortune has linked the name of a dead general to that of an electrocuted telegrapher, or, why not, the first name of a woman the soldiers dreamed about. This is the kind of mapmaking that attracts me, it's ridiculous and yet so human. It's rather like mapping dreams, with reality jumbled together, distorted, or subtly illuminated. Superimpose upon that dream map the surface map of ordinary place-names and you'll discover cruel ironies and bizarre connections. And that goes for the buried splendors of Babylon or Byzantium, Nemetocenna planted under Nemetacum, pagan sanctuaries underneath cathedrals. Over time, the science of surface maps becomes as boring as industrial photography. Moreover, I'm convinced you are wasting your time here. Try a little exercise for me. Look at any map at all and try to divine the subterranean map beneath it. Work without a method, be instinctual, like those people who try to analyze people's souls by looking at their handwriting.

The next day I had to excuse myself from my work. In fact I felt extremely lethargic. Taking the road toward Bailleul or Lens, marking off, collecting, taking notes. In addition, since all the sensitive species of lichens had been overtaken by disease, my report would be depressing. Studying the original map of diseased lichens closely, staring at it fixedly, a sort of parasitic thought took hold of me, I played a game of deformations. Squinting, I made the dark gray zone affected by acid rain waver, it began to undulate until it stretched from Dunkirk to Maubeuge to form an impenetrable front, beyond which I saw nothing. This brought back a memory of some cliffs, someone had grabbed me from behind and shoved me into the void. I folded the map again very quickly. Clearly, what he had called "deep cartography" only tells us something about ourselves. And this game was not without its dangers.

I found him next in the English cemetery, near the citadel. He was wandering alone amid three thousand white stones, engraved with crosses, perfectly aligned. He seemed a bit surprised to see me. Here we are, like

Alexander's two crows, he called at me in a jovial tone, but no one is going to follow us, that army is lost in the mustard-gas fumes. In spite of this welcome I saw that he was troubled. This always depresses me, he murmured, these young lives broken off, these stone-carved epitaphs, and all around us this obliviousness, lawns, birds, the town. Cemeteries make such gentle music that we don't hear the appalling things hidden inside them. In the Occident, interment has produced terrible misunderstandings, the crypt is conflated with the domicile, in the marble we engrave words like eternity. He had come to a stop in the middle of a row in front of a headstone that was like all the others:

> *Alexandre TYLER*
> *Rifleman*
> *King's Royal Rifle Corps*
> *4th March 1900*
> *2nd May 1917*
> *Gone but not forgotten*

We walked back in silence. Before returning to his room he told me he was thinking of leaving tomorrow, taking the sea route by Neuville-Saint-Vaast, Olhain, and other, smaller ports.

In search of what hidden trail? I asked him. He hesitated for a moment, then answered with a sad smile, the front line.

A final meeting took place in a hotel at Wimereux, four days later. Four days of lichens and fastidious annotations. I had been trying not to think about voyages from Brest to Siam, Alexander's crows, and the maps beneath maps. At Wimereux the old man was only a stick figure at the edge of the waves, even from a distance I recognized his way of standing in place for long periods, and then his rambling steps, like a solitary stork. Above him, under a cloudy sky, several seagulls with dirty white plumage glided in slow, sovereign flight. Tyler was, as usual, happy and dreamy. I matched my steps to his. How are your lichens coming along? he asked me. Not very well, I answered him, but I'm afraid no one will care. We sat on a large flat rock facing the sea.

Let's try a little exercise in forgetting, he proposed to me. Let's forget your lichens, let's forget the train that brought us to this spot, let's forget the streets, the hotel, the rooms, let's erase them from our memories. We are now in an earlier century, an improbable border-time which still believes that England is at the head of a noble, all-conquering empire. One thinks of an ocean liner slowly passing by, with its plume of smoke. Now, let's leap a half-millennium ahead. England has just been reduced to a skiff at best. Farther out, on the fringes of the horizon, the great ocean is populated only with islands, Kilwa, Mombasa, Zanzibar, Goa, the Antillean archipelago, an island named Peru, an island named Brazil, like so many stars dotted on a map by some fantastical mariner. Let's forget those islands, let's dive back into the swamp of History, we are in the first century, you and I sitting on the shore, let's convince ourselves that right here is the end of the world, a few crazy scattered fishermen still risk their lives at various places along the coast, but they fear the open water, they keep their sails fragile, intentionally, because farther out abysses yawn and monsters threaten. Now let's stop imagining, let's contemplate what we actually see before us, the horizon line is gone, sky and sea unite in a common weft and here and there we see pretty turquoise colors sailing by. There. And that's the end of your forgetting lesson.

He was silent for a long while.

Are you really a cartographer? I asked him.

No more than you, he answered. It's hard to believe that you would let yourself be crucified by all those lines and grids.

Sunk in the sea up to their knees, two shrimp fishermen in thigh-high boots assiduously steeped their triangle-shaped net in the waves. We started strolling again. At one point the old man slipped his hand under my arm as if we were old friends. Who was Alexandre Tyler, dead at seventeen? I asked him. He seemed not to hear me. I have the impression you're searching for something, I persisted awkwardly. He planted his cane in the sand, sighed while narrowing his eyes, you always end up talking to me about yourself.

Doubtless it is our destiny, he murmured later as we walked against the wind back toward the hotel, we are possessed by our ghosts, and I heard in his grave voice how much those words had cost him. The city streets bore the names of other cities, names of generals, and at the sign of the hotel the first name of a woman all the soldiers dreamed about. As dinner ended he wrote his address on the corner of a paper napkin, he told me, I will be leaving tomorrow, well before dawn, you will still be asleep, come and see me in Ipswich some day. And stop fighting with yourself, he added in a whisper while pressing my hand.

The entire next day was gloomy. In spite of myself I looked for him. I thought I saw him on the beach among the other figures. I imagined him elsewhere staring at the horizon, occupied with one of his exercises in forgetting or seeing. By evening he was still a gnawing voice, an accent dripping in a thicket of whispers.

Two days later I took the coastal train north. A feeling of dread made me go to Bray-Dunes where there was a storm. I went by taxi from Bray-Dunes to La Panne. Through all the lightning the driver recklessly drove his old carcass of a Mercedes, whose meter sounded like a time bomb about to explode. At La Panne the esplanade was being flattened under the downpour. And in the first restaurant past the border there was a terrible din made up of voices and traces of both music and the sound of raindrops on the awning of the veranda. And yet, nothing was different, everything was like anyplace else, identical, the same customers with vacant stares, perched on barstools, a rubicund barmaid, an aroma of fried fish, and the horizonless sea, sometimes brown, sometimes dark gray, behind the curtain of rain. I asked for stationery, I wrote:

> *Dear Mr. Tyler,*
> *Bad weather here.*
> *I'm abandoning my maps.*
> *I'm coming back.*
> *Someday I will definitely need to speak with you.*

It rained. It rained forever. It's a sure thing that the lichens in this country will be sicker than ever.

Woman in a Landscape

After a work by Marie Desbarax

Ever since that spring, she has been alert, she feels so free. Often she wanders over to the windows, the slightest pretext is enough, a sudden burst of light, a blue mist, an ooze of sunshine squeezed between two boughs, and she's gone again. You could trail her, it isn't hard, she always goes back to the same place. It's an ordinary place, a more or less simple haven in nature, neither flourishing garden nor fallow ground, *a few sloping prairies, rows of poplars*. There, see her there, very small at the foot of a tree, bowed over her white sheet like a scribe absorbed in interpreting the wind. Unless you lose her completely in the scenery, her distracted stare, her vagabond steps, among those tree trunks emaciated by the sun.

Some people are haunted by a face, others return indefatigably to places they remember, they are pilgrims in this world, tireless surveyors, this woman is in love with a landscape, he is her earthly lover, she's maddened, captive. It is enough for her to know she will see this small out-of-the-way spot with her own eyes or to hear her own voice breaking as she recounts the fact that she has been there. To you it would not look like anything, just an acre or two of land by the road, *a few sloping prairies, rows of poplars*, yet a woman keeps going there again and again to find and lose herself, she explores strange corners, abruptly embracing the interlacing of curves and edges, and the new perspective she's gained makes her reel with amazement.

Crazy, no doubt about that. She wants to sleep there. What she's looking for there is something that will nurture her being, at the very heart of the landscape, there where instinct whispers inside her, a gentleness resonating with my own gentleness, a terrestrial power to root me there. She turns herself into fox, rat, mole, or grouse, all familiars of her witchy presence. She turns herself into a collector. Her sketchbook is at the mercy of her greed for everything she sees. She fills it with sprigs, chestnut burs, pebbles, leaves whose veins protrude and which she will imprint upon the loamy ground then cook deep in an oven, inside a cave darkened by the shades of by-gone alchemists.

She sees musical scales in the alignments of trees, planted by human hands but married to the curve of the hills so tenderly (in echoes, in levels, in transparencies) that she hears music here, a harpsichord, prelude and fugue, twinklings and cascades of notes. She says, I want these obsessive rhythms, I want the sound of the wind in the poplars on my paper, I want these rustlings, these murmurs. Pick up the dead leaves, rub them to dust between your fingers, I want that sensation, she says. Crazy.

She sets her easel in the ground. She sets her square of white canvas beneath the unfurling sky. Time passes, she goes back. In April she watches for the light, in June the sparks, in July a field ablaze with glowing crystals, in November the golden boughs, under winter sunlight the bare plow furrows, bones. For everything is here, she says, in this landscape, everything she needs to nourish her eye, to quench her thirst, to feed her flesh, there is space to see through, and mystery for our human yearning after shade, and vertigo for our thoughts, because everything in this landscape changes from moment to moment, she claims, and the more she stands still the more she helps bring about this spectacle of continual blossoming, the earth's slow irruption, those cloaks of colors overlapping with the months, metamorphoses bleeding into each other, days chasing days, nights ripening the tomorrows they will never see, the circular advance of time.

And when I watch her as she paints, I see her pyromaniac eye, the light catches fire between her fingers, ignites the dry timber, sets the horizon aglow. And if later she darkens, playing now with earthly stuff, making a wellspring out of a gorge, I glimpse the same fevered absence in her eyes, like a child with mud-streaked cheeks doing just what she's been forbidden to do, plunging gleefully into the muck, the mire, the miasma. Higher up, the edges blur at the fringe of the sky, the trees are feathers in the wind, the water barely colors the aquarelle paper, in the stillness you can hear the touch of her brush upon the restive sheet.

But now and then the heavy presence of things, and now and then the hesitation of being, of being here without believing it, believing it without being here, that entire and primal stupefaction.

A woman looks at a landscape, at practically nothing, *a few sloping prairies, rows of poplars.* Transfixed, she goes back every hour of the day to find it again. She turns it into the sole destination of her journeys back and forth, endlessly she locates it on the map and traces there the shape of a mandala. I was born there, she says, it is my sheltered garden, my biblical paradise, the inexhaustible crucible of my childhood. I will die there too, you will find my body in the ranges of beech trees, you will rest my head on their hard bark, their consolation will be my happiness, I will never stop hearing the songs of their branches.

And when her hands pretend to be rearranging the charcoals or red chalks that she's brought back from down there, I feel her agitation, like her reticence, making these sacred relics meaningless, forcing me to invade the closed room of her love. But if, out of pure curiosity, I go to the place to look for myself, it feels to me that I'm somehow curled up with her, cozy and enclosed in the space inside her gaze, in the landscape's jealous immobility. Reminds me of a Chinese legend in which a painter got the idea of painting fog then ended up disappearing inside it. They never recovered his body, or his brushes, or his pencils.

Sometimes he still haunts the spot where he vanished, the legend goes, with his laugh or the frail ghost of his body. But he did leave behind a few sketches, a few canvases, proof that the whole story is true.

The End of Prose

To Francis Tessa
and to the friends of the l'Arbre à paroles

The organization had taken care of everything, bills in small denominations, an itemized itinerary of locations, and a perfectly plausible circumstantial introduction, thanks to which my presence would arouse no one's suspicion. What the organization had not accounted for was the fog, a kind of milky tar that stranded trains in the middle of open vistas and transformed the landscape into a scene of floating islands and evanescent bridges. These regions seemed cut off from the world, the rare inhabitants whom the fog had not engulfed stuck out along the quays like awkward specters of slumber, in that state of quivering emptiness which is called expectancy and which, little by little, hollows our lives like ancient tree trunks. Truth be told, I for one no longer expected much of anything. This case would be like all the ones before it, my report would circulate for a while among the highest levels of the organization, every page of it marked, underlined, initialed, finalized, and soon enough I would forget I had even written it, the way I would forget this country swamped in fog, where trains pulled up to deserted stations, haunted now and then by a loudspeaker's raucous squawk. Two things, nonetheless, awakened my attention. The first was intriguing: though the organization had planned my voyage down to the slightest details, it remained mute as to the subject of the report I was supposed to write. In addition, no due date had been set, and a fearsome little sentence in my orders left me at complete liberty *to hand in a report or else to hand in nothing.* This latitude was disconcerting, since the organization always delimited the purpose of each investigation quite inflexibly, invariably posed precise questions, and detested indeterminacy above all else. A second detail would have put me all the more on guard, had I noticed it at first. In the bundle of documents I had been furnished, the organization had not provided a return ticket. My journey was strictly one-way.

The man who came looking for me at the station was a short, bearded guy with a harsh voice and scorching eyes. He called himself Threerivers and claimed to work for the "charitable organization" whose name had appeared in large letters on my orders. The organization having prepared our meeting meticulously (I was to be, they had said, a writer in residence, I was writing a novel), he opened up the doors of his institute to me immediately and wholeheartedly. It was, at first glance, a run-down flophouse, with a sign reading, simply, the Poets' House, apparently an old girls' school in which they had now sequestered a few straggling boarders to take on the hazardous work of printing poems, hand-sewing folios, and stacking broadsides in cardboard boxes in case some distant collector took an interest. On the building's third floor, Threerivers, who was inexhaustible on the subject of his organization's exploits, could be seen painted as a Cardinal by some loony portraitist. I didn't see any point in inquiring into the meaning of the poems he published, they were, at a glance, full of nothing but pointless digressions and indulgent juxtapositions, all incongruous and chimerical, ground out in fits by some diseased mind or a writing-machine whose *random* switch had been flipped.

There was something fishy about it all. Fortified by all of my experiences, acquired in the bosom of the organization, I had a hunch from the very start that this so-called Poets' House was most likely a front for subversive operations the nature of which I swore I would file a report upon that same evening. Which is to say that doubt had not yet begun to set in, I fell back on the likely enough possibility that the report I was intended to write, and the question which the organization had not felt necessary to specify for me, hinged upon some nefarious activities on the part of Threerivers's collaborators. Via the chambermaid at the hotel where they had by some means arranged for me to stay, I was able to send a brief but already conclusive message to my superiors, in which I listed at least three illicit activities currently underway at the infamous house: one, recycling of public refuse; two, printing of obscene materials; and three, counterfeiting of money (evidence of which I had spotted under one of the numbered cardboard boxes). Further confirming this last item, Threerivers had prevented me from visiting his cellars, from which rose the incessant racket of rotary presses. The portion of the iceberg as yet submerged, in sum. Aboveground they appeared to be printing poems, in the basement they were cheerfully printing money, which was laundered somehow on its way up.

Alas, things weren't so simple. A first complication had already arisen when, on the day after my arrival, I was introduced to a writer, she too in residence at the Poets' House and lodging at the same hotel. This consumptive-looking woman affirmed that she came from a foreign country and had been working for several months on an extremely long poem. Her voice rasping as though coming to us from beyond the grave, she claimed to compose only four or five lines a day, and feared that she would never finish her work. Her agonizing manner of speech contrasted with her particularly colorful attire, fur muffs, silks, lace, and translucent veils that she wore with a mixture of disdain and nonchalance, like her nom de plume, Graziella. But her business card proved to be as terse as mine, and I read there clearly enough the handiwork of the organization, suspecting very quickly that my assignment to this case, added now to her own, had been planned by our hierarchy according to the accepted method of double infiltration, wherein two investigators who are essentially strangers are sent on the same mission in order to compare notes and likewise serve as useful diversions for each other, when their activities might otherwise appear suspicious. One writer in residence might seem a curious thing, but two writers in residence are a cross-cultural enterprise, they're there to have a multicultural experience, do research into transnational literatures, they can hold forth on Stendhal, Dante, Flaubert. Yes, our cover story was perfect.

As for transnational literatures, this amounted to diplomatic pleasantries more than anything, the organization having taught us to avoid any subjects that might cause our masks to slip. Questioned about my own literary work, I replied that it was a spy novel, after all this was the only genre where I had some expertise. Graziella, who must have grasped the allusion right away, seemed to shrug it off, but this information still managed to land in Threerivers's ear, and from that day onward he felt obliged to ply me with anecdotes on the subject of espionage, and to air his erudition at great volume. Whether it was Zopyrus (who hacked off his nose and ears to enter

Babylon) or the teachings of Sun Tzu on the hierarchy of secret agents (indigenous, undercover, double, sacrificial), the little man knew it all and I gnawed my knuckles for having gotten him started on this track. When at the end of our drunken dinners he finally stopped regaling us with the ruses of Caesar, the subtleties of Xerxes, or the intrigues of Richelieu, he let himself fall to dreaming of a utopian world, no longer making the slightest mystery of his criminal activities, even to the point of mentioning highly dangerous personal projects, such as the creation of *cells of poetic action*, similar to urban commando units capable of striking at a moment's notice, no matter where. Graziella, who could not hold her red wine, seemed indifferent to these revelations as I feigned being won over to our host's cause while mentally noting down the details of his conspiracy. Impassioned by the interest I showed him, Threerivers introduced me to his accomplices, all ostensibly men of letters, and again we found ourselves at table, discoursing together on the final preparations for their cultural revolution. At the end of these banquets, I was showered with gifts, poetry collections, and broadsides, all clearly subversive under their veil of meaningless babble. This roundabout incitement to rebellion called for exposure without delay. I placed all the evidence in an envelope that I left in care of the chambermaid, so she could alert the organization as soon as possible. And I waited for what would come next.

Strangely, this little go-between, a girl with blonde curls who was cute enough but made nervous gestures and had a fierce look about her, took my documentation in silence without giving me anything in return. That was when I began to get nervous. Stemming from the organization itself, this silence stretched from day to day, then from week to week, and ended up nibbling away, one by one, all the private certainties I had built up throughout the several decades of my career. This silence felt related somehow to the fog that drowned, every morning, this fluvial valley whose verdant plains my superiors had praised to me so highly. And it was mired, too, in Graziella's stare, washed out and absent, as if gutted by dreams, phantom barges half sunk beneath that long poem that she claimed slumbered in her black notebook day and night, crying out for her until her energy was entirely sapped. Though I fed her numerous lines, fleeting clues as to my cover, heavy-handed allusions to my so-called literary project (espionage), she watched them pass like trains across a landscape, walling herself up behind a haughty and infinitely weary pose, then leaving me without a word to return to her room. Over time, the long poem even won out over her multicolored scarves, her dazzling accessories, the clothing that she had formerly shown off, she was fading by the day. Writers are lonely stars, I said to Threerivers in her presence, they don't try to make contact. And the little man grinned through his beard, bidding us, out of pure malice, not to lose heart.

After several months had passed, for time had no meaning in this region, I felt I needed to bring in some evidence, I felt cut off from my chain of command, I paced the hotel's hallways endlessly and there was nothing left for me to do but leaf randomly through the folios from Poets' House with no idea in mind besides killing time, the way one unstrings a necklace of pearls solely for the pleasure of watching them roll away in all directions. I swear that, in the empty state in which I'd found myself, certain conjunctions of words made me feel dumbstruck or dreamy, and a curious music began to draw my ear, inflected with something *overheard*. But I repressed whatever it was very quickly because my memory has never been very good and introspection depresses me. In those days, long as white nights, I clung to each random appearance of the chambermaid, and to what traces of enigma still remained in Graziella's eyes. One day, transfixing her with a relentless stare, I announced to the poet that I knew everything about her and that there was no way she could not be aware of this fact, so let's end this masquerade. She stared at me with surprise, then with a hint of pity, but her lips stayed sealed. That evening I burst into her room once more and begged her to answer me, do you understand, I shouted, do you understand that they're waiting for us? She was lying on her bed, preoccupied with rereading one of the many broadsides that Threerivers had given us as gifts. I'm searching, she answered with her otherworldly accent, I'm searching, and she plunged back into her reading. This little event took on great importance, for it revealed a path, however tenuous. I went back to my room and reread what I had perhaps skimmed too quickly, like an impatient bloodhound, with a feverish itch to flush out misdeed or malfeasance. And that day brightened a bit, for I finally thought I understood why the organization had responded to my warnings, my evidence, my calls to action with such a profound silence. Perhaps they were simply asking me to read more deeply in order to shed light on the more covert activities going on at the Poets' House, even more covert than the covert activities it practiced in broad daylight. This illumination was, alas, of brief duration, since, the next day, the fog, which had been curled up somewhere, waiting, came back to blur shapes and strangle sounds in the valley. I read, understanding nothing,

> *While Betelgeuse dreams*
> *above the melee,*

or indeed,

> *The moon knocks with its silver skin*
> *on the doors of silence,*

and these words hob-

bled me gently, embedded themselves at the back of my head l so that I was unable to dislodge them, or translate them, still less to crack their code for my report to the organization. They ended up possessing me, like sly poltergeists, playing little games to set me onto the wrong track, and I felt as strong a need to forget them as I did to go back to them again and again, with no way to slake the improbable thirst they had stirred in me without my knowledge. While Betelgeuse dreams, even as I slept the words churned through me, *while Betelgeuse.*

Adding to my trouble, Threerivers insisted on enriching my research material on espionage with an ancient opus concerning the great cryptographers of history, such as the alchemist John Dee, or the Abbé Trithemius, author of the *Steganographia* or Book of Secret Writing, subtitled *The Art of Making One's Will Known to Persons Elsewhere.* Right away I took this as a valuable sign, I lost myself in conjecture, then vain attempts at transcription and decoding, I had to keep reminding myself that they were indeed covering something up here. Graziella vanished while I exhausted myself running down this false lead. She is no longer with us, Threerivers confirmed to me without further explanation. I pushed open the door of her room to see for myself, and discovered her colorful clothing lined up on hangers and floating lasciviously in the breeze. Not far away, her black notebook was planted in plain sight on the desk, invaded by a cramped thin illegible scrawl, which stopped abruptly in the middle of a page. A few days after Graziella, the little blonde maid disappeared in turn. I never saw Graziella's wild, distracted eyes again, and my sole link to the organization went with her. Henceforth, the hotel seemed more deserted than ever, the dining room glacial, the last remaining bellboy, the last receptionist shaking their heads with the stupor of automatons while the fog kept thickening behind the windowpanes, bathing the corridors in an anemic glow and discouraging the slightest impulse to go outside, the roads, the highways, and even the path that led to the Poets' House being dissolved, henceforth, in the same white molasses. At certain moments I could have sworn I was inside a trans-Arctic ocean liner entering the frozen zone, at other moments I hallucinated faces framed in the windows, I heard myself shouting from the top of a blind staircase, and I sought refuge in my room where the rereading of the poems ended up dissolving the small amount of serenity I still had left. In reaction to this crisis, I sat back down at my worktable and forced myself to draft for the organization an even more definitive version of the report I had already definitively finalized. But the sentences died before I could complete them, blank spaces blossomed between the words, which played with their own associations like silvered papers catching reflections of sunlight, and I was led against my will back to the poems and poets, I let myself tumble onto the bed, I slid down the slopes of those slim volumes, I plunged with dismay and delight back into that other writing, and I no longer became indignant when I read:

> *The solar system could be*
> *taken hostage*
> *by something even more immeasurable.*

Threerivers, who came on regular visits the way one comforts a prisoner in his jail cell, rejoiced in my new attitude toward poetry, he made encouraging if sibilant comments that I stewed over long after he went away. That is how you venture from the confines of the novel, he consoled me, you begin to accept the void, you are still inside the white cocoon of metamorphoses but you are learning how to unlearn it. And he brought me new texts published by his press, and I read, as if I had written it myself, this composition by Laozi,

> *The veil of light*
> *appeared cloudy*
> *The bright whiteness*
> *appeared dim*,

suddenly reminding myself of an old story we used to tell each other during our training, according to which the organization's employees always disappeared in the course of their final mission, becoming entirely one with their disguises, like mountain climbers in love with the peaks, who can sleep for eternity on a pillow of snow at eight thousand meters in the air. Immediately troubled by this memory, I opened up to Threerivers, I admitted everything to him, my deception, my terrible misgivings about literature, and, worst of all, my membership in the organization. He didn't seem to believe me at first, besieged me with questions, then finally shrugged it off by mumbling something that it took me a while to make sense of. It's true, all poets are double agents, he said, without suspecting the importance which that little sentence would hold for me. It illuminated everything, I told myself later that night, that makes everything perfectly clear, no return ticket, the fog all around and even the apothegms of my host when he'd welcomed me, the silence, the exhalation. On the day following that restless night, I felt a new strength rise inside me. Colors appeared in the frames of the windows and I distinctly heard, through the floor of my hotel room, a snatch of crystalline music that opened the boxes, the attics, the souvenir chests of my distant childhood. A strange liberty impelled me to sneak into Graziella's room, she who, in her absence, had now taken on the qualities of a misunderstood pixie. And I let myself roll in her sheets still imbued with perfume while my eyes inventoried her diaphanous gowns on their hangers. When I'm feeling better, I told myself, I will sit down with her black notebook, I will couple my large handwriting with hers, and when her long poem is finished, I will dedicate it to Threerivers, so that he will clutch it to his chest and print it up deep in the caves of the Poets' House, in the thunder of rotary presses, and who cares if later on the pages come loose in the wind, for the wind is the reader of all such things, who cares if the earth turns far away from me like some blue orb, I know that from now on my happiness will stay right here, in this project of choosing one word and then another, and the space separating them, thereby stretching out the thread until the very last word, which I will write trembling with joy and apprehension, a final trace across the blankness of the sky.

The quotations in "The End of Prose" are from Théodore Kœnig's *Envols de nuit*.

On Horseback upon the Frozen Sea

To Francis Martens

" 'I give you half a quarter of an hour,' answered Blue Beard,
'but not a minute more.' "

CHARLES PERRAULT

A dream place, Nathanaelle wrote me, detailing for
me in her beautiful slanted handwriting the furnished
manor house that she had just rented for a trifling price,
inventorying that refined and rustic interior with its
eggplant-colored jute carpets, its Spanish-style table, its
wrought-iron chandelier and the armoire made with
handles of wild cherrywood from the Loire Valley. Not
to forget the exquisite scent of the hearth permeating the
rooms upstairs, she confided to me in that lengthy letter on laid paper, grained with an elegant watermark,
wherein I grasped the real meaning of my friend's mi-
nutiae, her need to describe everything as if thereby put-

ting it in a symbolic order, everything having to be in its place, the curtains matching the jute carpets, the Spanish table centered beneath the chandelier and enhanced with a bouquet of fresh-cut flowers, while I pictured, floating through those rooms and just as harmonious within them, her beautiful figure making a sweeping campaign, smoothing out a piece of lacework here or moving a candlestick there, nothing ever being left to chance in the home of this woman who had taken a vow of elegance the way others take one of poverty, confiding to me in exacting detail a description of even the slightest of her furnishings as if the secret of our friendship resided in such meticulous description, covering the entire page, into the margins, except for the last sentence, which chimed joyously, like a promise, *I've gone on far too long but you know my fondness for old houses, to live in one is truly the art of living, when I'm finally done with my unpacking it will be my great pleasure to invite you here as my guest.*

But nothing in this world is ever free. If the rent on the manor was so low, Nathanaelle explained in her second letter, it was due to a strange clause whereby the renter could not make use of the main room immediately above the ground floor. The rest of the house more than made up for this small sacrifice, my correspondent consoled herself, adding with good humor that *being unable to come into this room* was not especially onerous to her and that ultimately she liked the idea that there was a locked door somewhere. In this, I recognized quite clearly my friend's enigmatic character, her desire for the perfect ambiguity. It was a fact that we had known each other for a long time and after all those years had not yet gotten around to addressing each other informally, as *tu*. The formal address was entrenched between us like a first line of defense, a dam against all likely intimate outbursts, and later a game that heightened our complicity. This was woven from secrets of no importance, Nathanaelle spared me no detail of her day-to-day life, she saw me as a confidant always willing to listen, a man whose feminine side she claimed to love and who, mysteriously excluded from the realm of desire, enjoyed the added advantage, for her, of not being a woman, hence a rival, and of not being a suitor (but what made her so certain of that?). Those nights when I saw her home after the theater, we kissed on the cheek then she waved to me faintly as she turned away and quickly tumbled back into the darkness. She never told me anything about her love affairs. I don't believe anyone had the last word on her, in this sense her mystery remained scrupulously guarded. *Ultimately I like the idea that there is a locked door somewhere.*

The third letter dwelled on her landlord, a person whom she portrayed as odd, rather unsociable, marked by that seeming harshness which often characterizes loners. Here is a man, she wrote me, whose silent presence cannot leave you indifferent. And if he had forbidden her that main room, this must be, she reasoned, due to a private wound of some sort, a grief most likely, the fact of having once lived with someone in this house but still unable, now, to turn the page. This secret was like a shadow on his face, which was handsome but glaring, as if carved in stone. Yet, despite appearances, the man proved himself charmingly obliging, attentive to the least of her wishes and determined to maintain the garden himself, which relieved her of an unpleasant task. So everything was going well enough in her new lodgings, the laundry room having been remade into an atelier, and she was able to walk past the forbidden room without paying it the slightest attention, as if it were an architectural extravagance or the walled-up sanctuary of a temple. In spite of this oddity, or perhaps because of it, the house grew more and more charming by the day, from the parlor to the loft, from the blue-marble-tiled kitchen to the old-fashioned guest room (her room now) whose view was simply unassailable. Try to picture, she concluded, a bed of ancient roses, and beyond that, between the shifting boughs of an old walnut tree, the green slope of a meadow, *this too is a home, a place from which one's eye can go roaming.*

A few days later, I heard her voice on the phone. This direct connection finally let us recover that tone of light banter of which she was fond. I was moved by her call, as since she'd chosen to bury herself deep in the country she had slid toward the periphery of my life, and her letters, always too literary, only added to that distance. Over the phone, however, I thought I could detect the thin timbre of her depressive episodes, her voice seemed a bit too chipper, haunted by nervous laughter, as if she was struggling with some inner sadness. Furthermore, she ended by mentioning some problems of adaptation, the fact that she still didn't feel at home in her new environment, decidedly not very conducive to solitude, reading, or quiet evenings. And when I insisted on coming to visit her, I felt as though she had been waiting for this and nothing else, being free the very next weekend and the forecast calling for superb weather.

Her abode resembled a small farmhouse more than a manor, it was a long edifice, invaded by ivy and surrounded by a perfectly cultivated garden, wide well-mown lawns, thick towering hedgerows whose amber tints harmonized with early autumn's yellow and fawn colors. Nathanaelle emerged from the house all smiles, wearing a dress that day the color of wine lees that made the livelier red of her lips sing out. In these new surroundings, under the wrought-iron chandelier described in her letter, at the foot of the Spanish table, I found her again as I had always known her, beautiful, distracted, and irrepressibly talkative, ferreting through her purse for her ultra-light cigarettes and intoxicating me with a thousand details of her new home. Only in her eyes, more sunken than usual, did I seem to read something fleeting, but likewise burdensome, as if my visit was causing her some apprehension. Happily, the pleasure of seeing each other again quickly enough dispelled this awkward impression. We sat down to eat, we had a good laugh at the assortment of daggers, krisses, dirks, cutlasses, and stilettos that garnished the hearth and stood out like fireworks against the lovely engravings, framed under glass and adorning the other walls of the room. I have not touched the landlord's collection, Nathanaelle explained to me, even though he's never said not to, at least in so many words. Do you know that there's a declaration of love engraved on the sheath of that kris? Entirely authentic. A declaration from him to you? I asked in a whisper. I still can't read the old Balinese, she replied with lowered eyes, then changed the subject. After lunch, she was eager to show me the whole house, from the cellar to the gables and down to the smallest cupboard. Passing the forbidden room she didn't refer to it by any sort of name, her long hand simply glided across the oak of the door and without looking at me she whispered, this is it. The room must have taken up the largest portion of the floor, but I didn't dare point this out to her. Outside the house, I noticed the twin braces of the closed shutters and my eye was irresistibly drawn to that sealed-off part of the building, as if eager to consume some inviolable secret. Nathanaelle wore her high boots and wrapped herself in her black cape, whose collar hid the lower half of her face. We followed a path leading toward the tree line, then we started to walk deep into the woods, until our conversation was increasingly punctuated by silence and the crunch of our footsteps on dead leaves. It was that hesitant hour at the end of day. The distant baying of a roebuck echoed through the deep forest. At one point, Nathanaelle grazed me with her hand, then regained her composure, let's go back, she said, let's go back.

During supper (game and a wild-berry compote) the wine relaxed us, we talked more about the landlord, his name was Brod, she found his eyes abnormally bright, his way of moving like a large animal's, his physiognomy like an old warrior's, his skin was tanned by the sun. He had been a surgeon in Africa but had not practiced since his return more than ten years previously. The taste with which he had furnished the house bore witness to a certain artistic sensibility, unless it was the work of that Madame Brod whose memory haunted the dwelling, and in whose name various shopping catalogs still regularly arrived in the mailbox. After tentative inquiries around the neighborhood, Nathanaelle had gradually begun to piece together the portrait of a young lady with reddish-blonde hair and very pale skin, who had once lived as a recluse behind the windows of the dining room where we were eating, and who went out only to walk a young stallion whom she kept at the nearest stable. Her image was beautiful but furtive in her neighbors' memories, they supposed the woman had been foreign (Hungarian, Russian, Polish?) for she spoke to no one, and yet her disappearance was keenly felt long after her departure, everyone immediately recalling the young horsewoman of the manor and lamenting her absence, much as they treasured those rare traces that she had left behind. I haven't given up on having the last word in this story, Nathanaelle confided with fire in her cheeks, for although Monsieur Brod is a taciturn man, he does not refuse a coffee after his hours of gardening, and I feel that little by little he is letting himself become more sociable. She didn't confide anything more on the subject, but I felt that she was troubled, perhaps already seduced, reminding myself more than once that Nathanaelle could be quite ravishing when she put her intimate emotions, her excesses, on display, but that none of this beauty was meant for me, this was the price of our friendship, earned through hard struggle over time and become, by now, almost natural. If I had, to be sure, entertained the thought of making an overture now and then, it was only to tell myself morosely that our relationship would not survive losing its way in the waters of desire. Routinely, and as if to underscore this same conclusion, she liked to praise my gift for listening, my availability, my infinite patience. In her rare declarations, always drunken, I was her cosmic, or karmic, twin, therefore a brother, we dwelled within the ineffable. At the close of that evening, I learned the circumstances of how she had met Brod, he had commissioned the restoration of an étude by Klimt from 1913, he was an art collector and bought other things besides antique knives. Such a man would know better how to seduce her, I told myself, for now I know everything, all about their first flirtations, but we can bet that when their love affair begins in earnest, I'll be shut out at once.

Since she occupied the only bedroom (the old guest room) in the house, I had to make do with a folding cot in the atelier. The room was cold, the moonlight carved white squares across the tiles, I was to spend several hours of insomnia with brief lapses of sleep. Through the ceiling I heard the plinking, then shuffling, of her footsteps, and in spite of myself my imagination looked again along the length of her legs, I pictured her up there, busy with her bedtime preparations, ablutions, and cosmetic treatments, yes, best to pursue that sort of imagery. A long while after midnight, the silence of the countryside was so fathomless that my thoughts echoed pell-mell like voices in a cave. There was a lamp on a table where the detached pages of a book she was working on were submerged in vats (there, again, I imagined her long white hands caressing the paper like diaphanous silk). Countless brushes were arrayed below a shining frame. Not far away an album was on display, where she exhibited before and after photos of her restoration work, there was the head of a sleeping woman signed Puvis de Chavannes and a pencil sketch by Klimt, a flabby woman, tunic pulled up, bare legs spread wide in a violently indecent pose.

I must confess something to you, she revealed at breakfast the following day. I don't know if I have the right to tell you, but it's too strange not to talk about it. And she told me how, one day the week before, unable to sleep because of fumes from freshly applied paint, she had the idea, at first silly, then exciting, of picking the lock on the forbidden room. She only really wanted to appease her curiosity. The door opened easily. The room, she recalled, contained an enormous bed covered with a lacework of raw silk, a vanity, and a chifforobe with white lead trim, as well as a bouquet of silk orchids, the only spots of color (purple, plum, lilac blue) inside that space, virginal, as if time there had stood still. The thought of stretching out on the bed came to her the next day at the siesta hour, a sudden, irresistible urge, because the sunlight there, sifting through the shutters due south, cast an alluring penumbra. Then, something extraordinary happened. She fell asleep right away, as quickly as a lightning strike, and immediately had a dream whose lucidity still troubled her. This dream was a picture she saw herself painting, at once a painting and the scene where she was painting it, a landscape of ice floes in whose foreground a woman in armor, riding a black stallion, was sinking gradually into the frozen sea. The visor of the rider's helmet was open and her face a mask of calm, a staggering beauty. Ever since this nap, which lasted only a few minutes, Nathanaelle had lived with her dream as with the most beautiful of the Old Masters' paintings, she never stopped replaying it in her memory, she had even attempted to draw it, acquiring the bizarre certainty that, behind that door, sealed once more, the space of the room was no longer off limits to her. I don't know if I have the right to tell you this story, she whispered, while I observed a change in her expression, her distracted eyes, her smile turned inward, the slight palpitation of her lips. Then she sat down to breakfast without another word. At morning's end we went out strolling again in the direction of the woods, but hunters had besieged the area, gunshots cracked the hum of the day, we had to keep to the paved roads. We walked side by side, we spoke little but this time the silence embarrassed us, I was certain she was thinking about her dream again, the frozen beauty, the Old Master's brushstroke, all the rest was only landscape.

Three weeks with no news from her, a too brief phone call concluding with a lapidary *I'll write you*, then the tone of her letter betraying the fact that the situation had taken a new turn. Her writing seemed shaken by some kind of groundswell to which her sentences bore witness without revealing much of anything. Country life had begun to weigh on her, she wrote, the evenings had grown longer since they'd switched back to winter time, the villagers seemed as mistrustful of her as the rest of the world, she came to regret her home's irritating little noises, from then on every single weekend would be taken up with those hunts that had taught her to detest the roaming parties of armed, local notables and the impression of distant warfare that would haunt this and every future Sunday. Perhaps my lodging here was a mistake, she admitted, I wanted a summer manor, a green garden, not this lugubrious house where the rainy days make me inconsolable for God knows what absent thing. Toward the end of her letter, however, she forced herself to smile, I don't doubt this is only a sojourn in the void, she wrote, and she was looking forward to taking a trip into the city, making a date with me after a gallery opening she felt obliged to attend. I must speak to you about something, she added without any further word about it, the lack of any mention of the landlord made me suspect that this something had to do with him.

The evening of the show I found her very beautiful, some sort of distress had opened up her demeanor, abolishing that haughty reserve with which she ordinarily kept her entourage at bay. As was our habit after going to the theater, we again installed ourselves in the back of that smoky tavern, the waiter shouting orders to the bar and the kitchen. There, beneath the intimacy of a very yellow globe-light, she started to talk to me about a deep anguish that had begun to infiltrate her sleep. As if she had discovered a feeling of solitude or rather *exposure to the void*, which she had never known before. An impression, she told me, of being brutally vulnerable, the thought that the walls no longer sheltered her from the unknown, from unforeseeable prowlers, from too keen a sensitivity to things, from the savage presence of nature, the sort of random cruelty against which she had always felt herself protected. It's a bizarre story, she laughed after a period of silence, it's crazy but I have to tell you. And she confessed to me that she had returned to the room, an impish curiosity had driven her to search the drawer of the nightstand and there Nathanaelle found photos of a woman who, feature for feature, matched the woman from her dream. The same static beauty, the same pale, somewhat morbid countenance, the same timeless silence, and Nathanaelle added that the recognition was instantaneous, indubitable, and that this resemblance frightened her so much that she swore never to go into the room again. You can't put your finger on what frightens you so much, she whispered, but suddenly you find yourself unable to think of anything else, you feel that the interior of your self is no longer the same, you think of reality mingling with dreams, you invent senseless stories. And she held out her hand so I could hold it in my own, locking me into a kind of stupor. I don't know what she saw in me, or through me, but the set of her lips seemed to indicate that she was in thrall to something, a mix of terror and joyous abandon that didn't conform to what she'd just told me. I spoke some reassuring words, she listened to my voice in silence, suddenly we were all alone in the world.

Winter broke out in November, within a few days the frost ruined the sumptuous ostentation of autumn. And night gained dangerous ground. I wanted to see Nathanaelle again, I had wanted to from the first day following our tavern meeting, I felt as if something had happened between us or else far away from us, some other place was drawing her attention away, and for the first time she had consented to show her fragile side. I tried to reach her by phone but had no luck, perhaps she still hadn't gone home. I wrote her a letter whose almost offhand tone I regretted right away, a trace of our usual banter. She called me on the evening of that envoi, around ten or eleven o'clock, her voice was breathless, she said she was afraid to spend the night alone in the house and begged me to come and see her as quickly as possible.

When I arrived at her house the next day, she apologized for her panic on the phone, blaming her nervous exhaustion on the wind, which, blowing for two or three days, had rattled her terribly. The whole time she was helping me take my coat off, putting my valise away in her atelier, she spoke a number of very solicitous words, here

113

you are, everything is better now, if I ever needed real proof of your friendship I couldn't have hoped for more. But her voice was frail, trembling, and behind her polite smile I felt her desperation. It also seemed to me that something in the house had changed, all of the shutters were closed and everywhere a casual messiness, quite unlike her, held sway. That evening saw us seated again in the dining room, where, under the effects of wine, she finally dared to open up, to hold her eyes on me longer than usual and finally admit to me that she had grown frightened of her landlord. Her suspicions arose, she explained, on account of the house's former occupant, and these misgivings had led her to question the neighbors once again about that Madame Brod, whom they described as being lost in her dreams, eternally imprisoned, a woman always alone, they confirmed in the village, a young beauty whom the landlord had locked up like a possession inside his eighteenth-century manor until the day she abruptly disappeared. Around the time of her disappearance, the elderly woman next door even thought she heard screams during the night, but perhaps that was only in her mind. Regarding the man, the landlord, the rumors were just as unequivocal, they claimed he had been forbidden to practice surgery, they said he was obsessed with hunting, on several evenings they had caught him firing guns in his garden, digging holes or moving soil, they tried to recall the last time they had seen the enormous black hound he kept locked in his garage, they said the landlord had an evil look, treacherous and shifty, as if he were hiding something. Neither treacherous nor shifty, corrected Nathanaelle, but glacial, his eyes lie in wait for you, ambush you, strip you bare. And the whole time I was listening to her I lost myself among the daggers aligned on the wall above the mantel. The blades gleamed, the hilts displayed their Damascene markings, the dirk of a Nazi officer dangled in its black shoulder holster, while my friend bitterly regretted the liberties she had taken earlier around the landlord, who now came twice a day, using the garden as a pretext (the eternal tasks of cutting, snipping, clipping, scarifying) to lay siege to the house, prowling around until evening and seeking to keep his tenant trapped inside by way of his pretended vigils. When he's in the garden, stressed Nathanaelle, I feel him watching me through the window, it overwhelms me, I must close the drapes. And again her hand moved to seek out mine, again I saw in her eyes the same fearful and ecstatic look casting its strange veil over what she was confiding in me. *I love how strong you are*, she whispered. Then she admitted to me that she had been seized by a strange suspicion. In the forbidden room there was a mirror facing the bed, she was afraid that the landlord had hidden a surveillance camera there and that she may have been observed in her trespassing. It might be a crazy idea, she stammered, but I would like you to help me verify it. At this hour of night, we are probably safe in assuming that he won't be watching.

I didn't realize at first that she had a key to the forbidden room, at the time I paid no attention to this. When the door was opened, I was overcome by the odor, a mix of stale incense and cloying petals drawing us deeper and deeper inside. The room was cavernous, suffused and tinted pink by the light coming though the lampshade. The bed looked so vast it made me want to stretch out upon it, unless there really was some magic spell at work in that murky glow that made the fabrics seem especially velvety and caused the flasks on the table to glitter like stars. Hanging at a tilt on the opposite wall, an antique mirror reflected the taupe cotton bedspread. Taking it down wasn't difficult, it was an oval mirror ensconced in a stucco frame, which hid nothing more than a little dust. Put it back exactly in its place, insisted Nathanaelle, who already seemed to have her mind on something else. And when this had been done, she ordered me to sit on the bed, closing the door ceremoniously. Do you hear it, she whispered, taking pains to contain her nameless, restless agitation, do you hear the echo in here?

On the little folding cot in her atelier I watched the red numbers of the digital clock tick past, deducted from the small amount of sleep that was left for me. In the middle of the night, around four o'clock, I heard soft cries panting through the floor. It was Nathanaelle's voice, evidently, but I had never heard her utilize such a plaintive inflection, nearly whimpering, and with my name, it seemed to me, my name uttered like a summons. Illuminating my path with the flame of my lighter, I ventured down the hall, then the staircase, of the dark house. Upstairs I noticed that the door of the forbidden room was open. I remained staring through this fissure for a long time until I was sure that it was she, curled up tight, her arms clutching the bedspread wrapped around her, her face turned to one side in slumber.

I spent an atrocious night, she announced the next morning, I didn't shut my eyes for a second. She had emerged from an endless séance of ablutions in the bathroom, having wrapped herself in a blue nightgown that made her body look sensational. I didn't know if she knew about my nocturnal visitation, but I gave her a bouquet of smiles, sympathy, and solicitous words as if it would be forgotten soon enough. That day we undertook another long walk in the forest and I recall being startled as much as she by the sudden baying of a stag very close by. It was a powerful rale, raucous, imperative, which rose again a little farther out, then farther still, diverting our hitherto aimless stroll and succeeding in getting us lost in the deepest depths of those humid pine woods. Something futile and grave had attached itself to our doomed quest, futile because we feigned being in good spirits, grave because of the cry of the beast, that fevered, frightened call, as if love was tragically necessary, a matter of life and death. Along the way, Nathanaelle's mood changed often, at some moments somber and silent, more often loquacious, almost flippant, her gestures friendly. Under the cover of a brief physical contact (we ran for a little while, I held her hand while crossing a stream), I asked her with a casual air if she often slept in the forbidden room. She made me repeat my words, feigning stupefaction, swore to her gods on high that she had never gone back there, insisted that I must have dreamed it.

For supper she set candles on the table, then changed her clothes, reappearing in a clinging dress whose neckline exposed her shoulders, wide shores of bare skin that made me turn my head away every time I noticed her staring at me a little too fixedly, sometimes the propitiatory victim, sometimes the fickle mistress of a conversation that always seemed to slip through our fingers. The landlord didn't come today, I said. Perhaps he sensed your presence, she responded, accompanying her words with a strange smile. And our dialogue traced the thread of this wonderful conceit, between the fear aroused by the defrocked surgeon, this man who made women disappear, and the complicity Nathanaelle and I had found in being afraid of him. Wine flowed abundantly and enlivened our talk. At one point I was bold enough to ask if Nathanaelle had dreamed of the horsewoman again when she slept in the forbidden room. She seemed at a loss, eventually chose surprise, then a tone of gentle petulance, but why did I keep insisting that she *had* slept there? I stood my ground, swore I had seen her, I had not dreamed it. She countered that the nature of dreaming is to conceal from the dreamer the fact that he is actually dreaming. And thence, one thing leading to another, we launched into a friendly joust about reality and dreaming in which I admit I took some pleasure. In conclusion she conceded that one of us must be a somnambulist, and we clinked our glasses to this resolution of the conversation, with neither of us declared the winner or loser. A little later, she herself started in again, in a questioning tone, full of suppositions. Let us say that she had indeed slept in the room. And what if the landlord found out about this? And what if this house was a trap for women who were too curious? Had I ever looked closely at the blades of the daggers around the fireplace? And what if we went down into the cellar to see if he had recently been digging there? And what if he was standing right there in front of her, what would I do? Her glass was right up to her lips, she was devouring me with her dark eyes. I would make a shield with my body, I said. She laughed very shrilly, then slowly regained her composure, her eyes capsizing, sinking to the bottom of my own. I do like, she said with the voice of a little girl, *I do like how you said that.*

After dinner we no longer felt like pursuing this line of conversation, she pulled her chair close to mine, swaying first toward me then toward the record player, and soon we were rocking back and forth in each other's arms to a fuzzy blues song that sputtered nostalgia in deep raspy salvos. Now and then she let her head fall upon my shoulder, then tried to straighten me up to my full height, hold me, hold me tight, you lead the dance. When the music ended, she took a step back, reeled backward toward the void, then proposed with a sigh, *let's go.*

The door of the forbidden room wasn't even closed. Nathanaelle turned off the lamp at once and, scarcely remembering that it was there, we tumbled into the bed without a moment's hesitation. I searched for her face in the dark but it floated like a veil on the night wind. Her body, my body mingling with hers, that black voluptuous struggle seemed to feed upon an ancient, immemorial history, of which the years of our friendship, now that it was too late, were only a strange outgrowth. And I saw us on horseback upon the frozen sea, in the immense vertigo of the landscape, while her cries rang out, pierced by light laughter, as if she had become a little girl again.

I opened the shutters to let the morning light into the room. In truth it was very white, except for the lampshade and the spray of silk orchids. Nathanaelle didn't react to the light, she slept peacefully, her brow unwrinkled, as if entirely content. And her face floating high in the oval mirror resembled a tutelary angel's. When she opened her eyelids she looked at me and smiled. I've unlatched a shutter, I told her. She didn't seem worried. Does he sometimes come in the morning? She gave a big nod. Yesterday he didn't come, I said, but we're taking something of a risk. While you're here to protect me, she responded in a whisper, I am not afraid. And what if he's simply waiting for a propitious moment? What if he's lured us into this room to kill us both? She swept one finger across my lips to silence me. At the very least we would die together, she parried, still smiling. The light caressed her face in profile, her tender cheeks and her ingenuous eyes in front of the dark streak of the open door. Anyway, we would tell him nothing happened, her melodious voice continued, we would tell him, no, Monsieur Brod, nothing happened, besides we were never in the room, Monsieur Brod, we were never here.

FRANÇOIS EMMANUEL was born in 1952 in Fleurus, Belgium. After studying medicine, he took an interest in poetry and theatrical adaptation. His novel *La Question humaine* (translated as *The Quartet* in 2001) was adapted into an acclaimed film, titled *Heartbeat Detector* in English, in 2007. Emmanuel now spends his time as a writer and a psychotherapist. Since 2004, he has been a member of the Belgian Academy of French Language and Literature.

JUSTIN VICARI is a poet, critic, and translator. His first collection of poems, *The Professional Weepers*, won the Transcontinental Award. He is also the author of *Male Bisexuality in Current Cinema: Images of Growth, Rebellion, and Survival* and *Mad Muses and the Early Surrealists*.

Man in the Holocene.
CARLOS FUENTES, *Christopher Unborn.*
  Distant Relations.
  Terra Nostra.
  Where the Air Is Clear.
WILLIAM GADDIS, *J R.*
  The Recognitions.
JANICE GALLOWAY, *Foreign Parts.*
  The Trick Is to Keep Breathing.
WILLIAM H. GASS, *Cartesian Sonata
    and Other Novellas.*
  Finding a Form.
  A Temple of Texts.
  The Tunnel.
  Willie Masters' Lonesome Wife.
GÉRARD GAVARRY, *Hoppla! 1 2 3.*
  Making a Novel.
ETIENNE GILSON,
  The Arts of the Beautiful.
  Forms and Substances in the Arts.
C. S. GISCOMBE, *Giscome Road.*
  Here.
  Prairie Style.
DOUGLAS GLOVER, *Bad News of the Heart.*
  The Enamoured Knight.
WITOLD GOMBROWICZ,
  A Kind of Testament.
KAREN ELIZABETH GORDON,
  The Red Shoes.
GEORGI GOSPODINOV, *Natural Novel.*
JUAN GOYTISOLO, *Count Julian.*
  Exiled from Almost Everywhere.
  Juan the Landless.
  Makbara.
  Marks of Identity.
PATRICK GRAINVILLE, *The Cave of Heaven.*
HENRY GREEN, *Back.*
  Blindness.
  Concluding.
  Doting.
  Nothing.
JACK GREEN, *Fire the Bastards!*
JIŘÍ GRUŠA, *The Questionnaire.*
GABRIEL GUDDING,
  Rhode Island Notebook.
MELA HARTWIG, *Am I a Redundant
    Human Being?*
JOHN HAWKES, *The Passion Artist.*
  Whistlejacket.
ALEKSANDAR HEMON, ED.,
  Best European Fiction.
AIDAN HIGGINS, *A Bestiary.*
  Balcony of Europe.
  Bornholm Night-Ferry.
  Darkling Plain: Texts for the Air.
  Flotsam and Jetsam.
  Langrishe, Go Down.
  Scenes from a Receding Past.
  Windy Arbours.
KEIZO HINO, *Isle of Dreams.*
KAZUSHI HOSAKA, *Plainsong.*
ALDOUS HUXLEY, *Antic Hay.*
  Crome Yellow.
  Point Counter Point.
  Those Barren Leaves.
  Time Must Have a Stop.
NAOYUKI II, *The Shadow of a Blue Cat.*
MIKHAIL IOSSEL AND JEFF PARKER, EDS.,
  *Amerika: Russian Writers View the
    United States.*
DRAGO JANČAR, *The Galley Slave.*
GERT JONKE, *The Distant Sound.*

Geometric Regional Novel.
  Homage to Czerny.
  The System of Vienna.
JACQUES JOUET, *Mountain R.*
  Savage.
  Upstaged.
CHARLES JULIET, *Conversations with
    Samuel Beckett and Bram van
    Velde.*
MIEKO KANAI, *The Word Book.*
YORAM KANIUK, *Life on Sandpaper.*
HUGH KENNER, *The Counterfeiters.*
  *Flaubert, Joyce and Beckett:
    The Stoic Comedians.*
  Joyce's Voices.
DANILO KIŠ, *Garden, Ashes.*
  A Tomb for Boris Davidovich.
ANITA KONKKA, *A Fool's Paradise.*
GEORGE KONRÁD, *The City Builder.*
TADEUSZ KONWICKI, *A Minor Apocalypse.*
  The Polish Complex.
MENIS KOUMANDAREAS, *Koula.*
ELAINE KRAF, *The Princess of 72nd Street.*
JIM KRUSOE, *Iceland.*
EWA KURYLUK, *Century 21.*
EMILIO LASCANO TEGUI, *On Elegance
    While Sleeping.*
ERIC LAURRENT, *Do Not Touch.*
HERVÉ LE TELLIER, *The Sextine Chapel.*
  *A Thousand Pearls (for a Thousand
    Pennies)*
VIOLETTE LEDUC, *La Bâtarde.*
EDOUARD LEVÉ, *Autoportrait.*
  Suicide.
SUZANNE JILL LEVINE, *The Subversive
    Scribe: Translating Latin
    American Fiction.*
DEBORAH LEVY, *Billy and Girl.*
  *Pillow Talk in Europe and Other
    Places.*
JOSÉ LEZAMA LIMA, *Paradiso.*
ROSA LIKSOM, *Dark Paradise.*
OSMAN LINS, *Avalovara.*
  The Queen of the Prisons of Greece.
ALF MAC LOCHLAINN,
  The Corpus in the Library.
  Out of Focus.
RON LOEWINSOHN, *Magnetic Field(s).*
MINA LOY, *Stories and Essays of Mina Loy.*
BRIAN LYNCH, *The Winner of Sorrow.*
D. KEITH MANO, *Take Five.*
MICHELINE AHARONIAN MARCOM,
  The Mirror in the Well.
BEN MARCUS,
  The Age of Wire and String.
WALLACE MARKFIELD,
  Teitlebaum's Window.
  To an Early Grave.
DAVID MARKSON, *Reader's Block.*
  Springer's Progress.
  Wittgenstein's Mistress.
CAROLE MASO, *AVA.*
LADISLAV MATEJKA AND KRYSTYNA
  POMORSKA, EDS.,
  *Readings in Russian Poetics:
    Formalist and Structuralist Views.*
HARRY MATHEWS,
  *The Case of the Persevering Maltese:
    Collected Essays.*
  Cigarettes.
  The Conversions.
  The Human Country: New and

Collected Stories.
The Journalist.
My Life in CIA.
Singular Pleasures.
The Sinking of the Odradek Stadium.
Tlooth.
20 Lines a Day.
JOSEPH MCELROY,
Night Soul and Other Stories.
THOMAS MCGONIGLE,
Going to Patchogue.
ROBERT L. MCLAUGHLIN, ED., *Innovations: An Anthology of Modern & Contemporary Fiction.*
ABDELWAHAB MEDDEB, *Talismano.*
GERHARD MEIER, *Isle of the Dead.*
HERMAN MELVILLE, *The Confidence-Man.*
AMANDA MICHALOPOULOU, *I'd Like.*
STEVEN MILLHAUSER,
The Barnum Museum.
In the Penny Arcade.
RALPH J. MILLS, JR.,
Essays on Poetry.
MOMUS, *The Book of Jokes.*
CHRISTINE MONTALBETTI, *Western.*
OLIVE MOORE, *Spleen.*
NICHOLAS MOSLEY, *Accident.*
Assassins.
Catastrophe Practice.
Children of Darkness and Light.
Experience and Religion.
God's Hazard.
The Hesperides Tree.
Hopeful Monsters.
Imago Bird.
Impossible Object.
Inventing God.
Judith.
Look at the Dark.
Natalie Natalia.
Paradoxes of Peace.
Serpent.
Time at War.
The Uses of Slime Mould: Essays of Four Decades.
WARREN MOTTE,
Fables of the Novel: French Fiction since 1990.
Fiction Now: The French Novel in the 21st Century.
Oulipo: A Primer of Potential Literature.
GERALD MURNANE, *Barley Patch.*
YVES NAVARRE, *Our Share of Time.*
Sweet Tooth.
DOROTHY NELSON, *In Night's City.*
Tar and Feathers.
ESHKOL NEVO, *Homesick.*
WILFRIDO D. NOLLEDO, *But for the Lovers.*
FLANN O'BRIEN,
At Swim-Two-Birds.
At War.
The Best of Myles.
The Dalkey Archive.
Further Cuttings.
The Hard Life.
The Poor Mouth.
The Third Policeman.
CLAUDE OLLIER, *The Mise-en-Scène.*
Wert and the Life Without End.
PATRIK OUŘEDNÍK, *Europeana.*

The Opportune Moment, 1855.
BORIS PAHOR, *Necropolis.*
FERNANDO DEL PASO,
News from the Empire.
Palinuro of Mexico.
ROBERT PINGET, *The Inquisitory.*
Mahu or The Material.
Trio.
A. G. PORTA, *The No World Concerto.*
MANUEL PUIG,
Betrayed by Rita Hayworth.
The Buenos Aires Affair.
Heartbreak Tango.
RAYMOND QUENEAU, *The Last Days.*
Odile.
Pierrot Mon Ami.
Saint Glinglin.
ANN QUIN, *Berg.*
Passages.
Three.
Tripticks.
ISHMAEL REED,
The Free-Lance Pallbearers.
The Last Days of Louisiana Red.
Ishmael Reed: The Plays.
Juice!
Reckless Eyeballing.
The Terrible Threes.
The Terrible Twos.
Yellow Back Radio Broke-Down.
JOÃO UBALDO RIBEIRO, *House of the Fortunate Buddhas.*
JEAN RICARDOU, *Place Names.*
RAINER MARIA RILKE, *The Notebooks of Malte Laurids Brigge.*
JULIÁN RÍOS, *The House of Ulysses.*
Larva: A Midsummer Night's Babel.
Poundemonium.
Procession of Shadows.
AUGUSTO ROA BASTOS, *I the Supreme.*
DANIËL ROBBERECHTS,
Arriving in Avignon.
JEAN ROLIN, *The Explosion of the Radiator Hose.*
OLIVIER ROLIN, *Hotel Crystal.*
ALIX CLEO ROUBAUD, *Alix's Journal.*
JACQUES ROUBAUD, *The Form of a City Changes Faster, Alas, Than the Human Heart.*
The Great Fire of London.
Hortense in Exile.
Hortense Is Abducted.
The Loop.
Mathématique:
The Plurality of Worlds of Lewis.
The Princess Hoppy.
Some Thing Black.
LEON S. ROUDIEZ, *French Fiction Revisited.*
RAYMOND ROUSSEL, *Impressions of Africa.*
VEDRANA RUDAN, *Night.*
STIG SÆTERBAKKEN, *Siamese.*
LYDIE SALVAYRE, *The Company of Ghosts.*
Everyday Life.
The Lecture.
Portrait of the Writer as a Domesticated Animal.
The Power of Flies.
LUIS RAFAEL SÁNCHEZ,
Macho Camacho's Beat.
SEVERO SARDUY, *Cobra & Maitreya.*
NATHALIE SARRAUTE,
Do You Hear Them?

FOR A FULL LIST OF PUBLICATIONS, VISIT:
www.dalkeyarchive.com